THE COWBOY'S HONOR

LACY WILLIAMS

PART I

1

1905 - Denver, Colorado

Someone was pounding on the door. Emma Morris tried to rouse herself from a deep sleep, but it felt like swimming through molasses.

Bam, bam, bam.

All right. She was awake.

It had to be the middle of the night. Since she'd lost her sight two years ago, it was harder to discern the passing of time. She and her brother Daniel lived on a quiet residential street a few blocks from Denver's bustling downtown. In the mornings, there might be neighbor children playing games in their front yards or a housewife chatting with her chickens. Of an evening, there would be scents of whatever her neighbors were cooking and sometimes the sounds of families conversing through their open windows.

In the beginning, she'd strained her ears to listen to those voices talking over each other, and she'd grieved everything she'd walked away from. But even her grief had been dulled by time and distance.

Right now, it was completely quiet. Even the pounding that had woken her had stopped.

She grabbed her shawl from the chair at her desk and wrapped it around her, covering her flannel nightdress.

As she stepped out of her room and into the upstairs hallway, quiet, muffled voices met her ears. Cool air swirled around her feet. Daniel must've gone downstairs and opened the door. It must be an emergency. They never had middle-of-the-night visitors like this.

There was muffled sound and then an exclamation from Daniel.

"What is it?" she asked from the top of the stairs. She stood with one foot on top of the other to try and keep both feet from turning into blocks of ice.

"Go back to bed," was Daniel's distant response.

It sounded as if he were dragging something heavy through the house, toward the parlor. What in the world...?

Cold air still rushed inside the open door and up the stairs. Obviously, the door was standing open. Daniel was talking in a low voice, now in the parlor. Talking to himself?

Instead of returning to her room, Emma padded down the stairs.

She shivered against the draft and quickly reached out to close and lock the door.

Daniel never invited his clients home. He'd discouraged her from visiting his office. She knew he worked with difficult people, some criminals. Occasionally, he'd received a message and left on a mysterious errand late in the evening.

But never anything like this.

What was happening?

She moved on near-silent feet into the parlor. The rug beneath her toes meant she'd reached the edge of the room, and she stopped there, unsure.

"Daniel, what is going on?"

A low groan from across the room startled her. It hadn't come from Daniel.

"I told you to go back to bed." Her brother sounded exasperated.

He should know better by now than to order her around like that. It wasn't going to work.

He sighed. Maybe he'd realized the same thing.

"Who was at the door? Who is... that?" She didn't know what to ask. Was the person who had groaned injured?

"If you aren't going to go back to bed, then start some water boiling and bring some cloths. I need to staunch this wound until the doctor arrives."

She hadn't gotten an answer about who was in their home, but someone was wounded. She hurried to the kitchen to do Daniel's bidding.

It wasn't like her brother to prevaricate. He didn't want

her to know the identity of the injured person in their parlor.

Why the secrecy?

She stoked the fire by touch—it was habit after all this time—and put on a pot of water to boil. When she returned to the parlor with her arms full of cloths, the room was silent except for the sounds of two people breathing.

Daniel's breaths were deep and even. He must be sitting on the sofa, or maybe kneeling on the floor next to it. As she neared his side, she could hear the stranger struggling for breath. Whoever it was, each breath was shallow and almost sounded wet.

"What can I do?" she asked, laying the cloths on the low table next to the sofa.

"Pray. He's been badly beaten. At least one stab wound. Someone kicked him in the ribs. And he's got a lump on his skull. The doctor's coming, but..."

But whoever this was might not make it. The gravity of the situation felt heavy in Emma's middle.

"He?" she asked softly.

"Emma, I don't quite know how to say this, but... it's Seb White."

AT FIRST HE was only aware of darkness. Darkness and pain.

More awareness came in snatches.

Memories whirled through him, masquerading as dreams.

His adopted ma, Penny, serving a lopsided, half-frosted birthday cake when he'd been all of seven.

A voice he would never forget came from somewhere nearby. Why couldn't he see her? *"I'm worried that he hasn't woken up yet."*

Driving cattle with his pa. The wide open Wyoming sky above them and Jonas giving him a proud smile.

Holding a letter in his hands. An important letter. And then crumpling it into a ball and tossing it into a fire. Watching it burn.

Another voice he recognized, a man's voice. *"The doctor said the fever is burning away infection. If it doesn't fade soon, I'll fetch him again."*

There was a momentary sensation of bliss as something cool rested on his head and neck.

A whisper. *"Seb. Wake up."*

Last, a memory he'd buried so deep that he hadn't thought of it in years. He didn't know how old he was. A little tyke, that was for sure. *He was standing in a dusty street, his stomach howling with hunger pangs. Somehow he knew. That he was absolutely, terrifyingly alone. He called out for everyone he could think to call out for. A mama he no longer remembered. A papa. Had there been someone else? An older sister? He couldn't remember now. All he knew was that it didn't matter how much he cried, nobody came.*

It was that ugly memory from his childhood that forced him awake. When the pain hit, he wished he were still unconscious. His midsection was on fire. He'd definitely busted a rib or two. And something deeper than that, something on the inside wasn't right. His face ached. His head, too. Even his legs felt bruised to the bone.

It all rushed back to him in an instant. Tolliver's thugs —three against him. The beating he was pretty sure he wasn't supposed to have survived.

But against all odds, it seemed he had. He cracked one eye open. Where was he? If Tolliver had him locked away in a storehouse somewhere, he might wish himself dead.

Just the effort it took to open his eyes sent spears of pain ripping through his pounding skull. Morning sunlight was shining in the window decked by some kind of blue frilly curtains. A bookshelf filled with thick, leather-bound tomes lined one wall. There were fresh flowers on a sideboard. and he seemed to be lying on some kind of makeshift bed. A sofa, he realized. He was in a parlor he didn't recognize. He'd never been here before.

Was this one of Tolliver's properties? Seb's former boss was wealthy and had more than one house in Denver. What if the thugs had brought him here?

He had to get away from this place.

But when he tried to rise up on his elbows, shards of pain sliced through his midsection. He breathed fire.

Flat on his back again, he panted through the agony. Had he cried out? He couldn't be sure.

Footsteps approached and he froze, trying to settle his breathing. He closed his eyes, not wanting whoever was keeping an eye on him for Tolliver to know he was awake.

He heard steps. They faltered near the doorway, then continued closer. A skirt swished.

A woman?

He'd been around too many women growing up. There was no mistaking the sound.

He could overpower a woman and escape. Maybe. He was awfully weak.

Seb couldn't stand not knowing.

He opened his eyes the slightest bit. Kept his face smooth, hoping whoever it was would believe him still asleep.

And saw her.

Suddenly, all his intentions of pretending to be unconscious disappeared like leaves on a brisk mountain breeze.

His eyes flew open. Weakness that had nothing to do with his injuries immobilized his limbs.

It was Emma. *His* Emma.

No.

Not his anymore.

What was she...? He blinked a slow blink, trying to wake himself up. What was Emma doing involved with Tolliver?

She wasn't.

That knowledge loosed the cinch that had clenched around his chest since he'd come to. There was no way Emma—tenderhearted, couldn't-tell-a-lie-to-save-her-life Emma—was involved with Tolliver.

Which meant that somehow Seb had been delivered to her doorstep.

He flicked a glance at the rag and bowl on the low table next to him. *Emma* was taking care of him? Helping him?

Why?

His spinning thoughts had taken only the space between two breaths.

She was rounding the end of the sofa now, her slender form almost close enough to touch.

His heart beat a sluggish, painful drum in his chest.

His head was still pounding, and he couldn't make his thoughts line up.

How had he ended up here, in what must be Emma and Daniel's home?

Did Emma know who he'd been working for?

The last time she'd written, Emma had said she never wanted to see him again.

She bent closer, and soft, cool fingers touched his wrist. Her touch was there and gone so quickly that he wanted to weep. Even if his broken body had been able to move, he was frozen in place, barely breathing.

He tried to brace himself for her glance at his face. Would he see disgust in her eyes for what he'd become?

But when her gaze flicked to his face, it was unfocused. He wasn't even sure that she was really looking at him.

She straightened and moved across the room toward the window.

She hadn't said one word to him, though he'd been staring at her the entire time.

The pain of her dismissal rose among the physical pains rolling through his body.

He let the anger come because it was easier than feeling the turmoil inside.

Obviously, her feelings for him had not changed. Whatever small affection she'd felt for him before she'd left Wyoming was gone. Obliterated by what? Something he'd done? Or...? Maybe she'd never really cared for him at all.

How had he ended up in her house? Why was she caring for him, if she was so indifferent? Their families were connected—his brother was married to her sister—but he'd never planned to cross her doorstep when he'd come to Denver.

He'd never thought to have the chance.

He'd used his fists to get this far from home. Boxing and brawling his way through gambling dens and saloons until he'd reached Denver.

The parts of town where he made his living were far removed from this sun-filled, proper home.

How had he ended up here? The question repeated in his mind, but Emma was staring out the window now, and fierce pride kept him silent.

If she had nothing to say to him, then he certainly had nothing to say to her.

He didn't need her help.

Stubborn pride kept him still and silent on the sofa. He didn't want her to see how weak he was.

When she left, he'd get off this sofa—no matter how much it hurt—and walk out of there.

He studiously ignored the fact that he hadn't been able

to sit up only a few minutes before. His injuries weren't ideal, but he was still alive, wasn't he?

However, as the situation became clearer, he realized he was shirtless. A blanket covered his upper body, and when he shifted slightly, he felt the pull of what must be stitches on his left side beneath his ribs.

He experienced a swift recollection of a huge goon, a glint of metal in the moonlight, the slice of a knife and searing pain.

The memory brought phantom pain in addition to the burn he already felt, and he must've shifted somehow or made some noise because Emma's head turned slightly in his direction.

But her eyes were unfocused again. And she still didn't speak.

And he knew that he had to get out of here.

No matter if he was shirtless with no money to his name, no horse, and half dead.

As soon as she left the room, he'd go.

But since she was ignoring him anyway, he let his eyes slide closed. He'd just rest his aching head until she left.

Darkness dragged him under.

2

The slam of a door startled Seb awake.

Dusk was falling, the sitting room much darker, and he struggled for a moment through the pain until he remembered where he was.

And that he had no intention of staying.

The slamming door must've been a neighbor. It was quiet in Emma's home.

He craned his neck—ignoring the sharp pain in his head—to make sure she'd gone.

The room was empty.

As he listened, he could hear familiar kitchen sounds. Seemed she was making supper.

Time to go.

Except when he tried to push himself to a sitting position, those stitches in his side pulled and burned, making him gasp with pain. He went hot and then cold. His hands trembled as he scrabbled for a grip on the too-smooth sofa.

He was still horizontal when a door opened and then closed. Heavy footsteps moved away from him. Voices murmured from the other room. The kitchen, if his earlier guess had been correct.

It sounded like Daniel was home.

Unless...

Maybe Emma had married in the two years since he'd seen her.

The heavy footsteps returned. This time, the parlor door opened, and Daniel strode inside.

Seb ignored the beat of relief that swept through him. He no longer cared who Emma had in her life. Right?

Unlike the way Emma's gaze had glanced and bounced off of him, Daniel's direct stare landed right on Seb.

"You're awake." The man moved further into the room, standing near the foot of the sofa so Seb didn't have to strain his neck. He could've wept in relief.

"Help me up." Seb's voice was scratchy, unused.

Daniel shook his head. He was near the same age as Seb's older brother Maxwell. And Seb had been the recipient of a disappointed look—just like Daniel wore now—from his brother plenty of times.

"I don't think so. Not after all the work the doctor did to put you back together. Stop that."

Seb was struggling to a sitting position even as Daniel refused to help him.

He didn't make it. He lay back on the cushion, right hand crossing his body to clutch the wound in his side.

Daniel shook his head slightly, disgust clear in the twist of his lips.

Anger flushed Seb's skin hot. He hated that the other man was seeing him weak.

Daniel moved closer, and Seb reacted by instinct, twisting his body and throwing out one hand to protect himself.

Something softer than the disgust moved through Daniel's expression faster than Seb could read it. Concern? Compassion? But maybe he'd imagined it. Or blacked out for a second, because when he blinked, Daniel was holding out a glass of water to him.

Seb took it and drank greedily, flushing when some of the liquid escaped the glass and dribbled down his jaw to wet the collar of his shirt.

Just the effort of taking a drink exhausted him, and his head fell back as Daniel rescued the glass from his hand.

He was too weak to get up on his own, and Daniel refused to help him.

"What'd the doctor say?" he asked.

Daniel knew he was really asking *how long*? The other man's eyes glittered with some emotion Seb couldn't read. "The knife wound in your side was vicious. He was certain it would become infected—probably why you've been fighting a fever for four days. Broken ribs, bruising all up and down your body."

At Daniel's cold recitation, Seb could feel every pain mentioned.

"He was also worried about your head. You've got a contusion here"—Daniel pointed a long finger at his right temple—"that the doc said looked like had come from the wrong side of a heavy boot."

Seb didn't remember that. He'd gone down swinging, but it'd been three against one, and Ralph had had that knife. At one point he'd been knocked to the ground. He remembered the kick to his ribs. But he'd had his arms up, guarding his head.

He blinked away the memory. Daniel was still staring at him. Assessing him.

"You want to tell me what happened? Who jumped you?"

Nothing on earth was going to make Seb talk about what he'd been involved in or how he'd been ambushed.

"How'd I end up here?" He'd known Daniel and Emma lived in Denver. It was where he'd addressed those ill-fated love letters. Since his arrival, he'd stayed plenty far from their ritzy address. Daniel was a lawyer—and a successful one, apparently—and their house was in a fine part of town. Seb's business had kept him in the seedy corners of the city. Somewhere Emma would never be caught dead.

He hadn't meant to stay for as long as he had.

And now look where he'd ended up.

Daniel didn't answer. His calculating gaze remained on Seb.

Seb broke first. "If Tolli—" he cut off his words. Started

again. "If the thugs who tried to kill me know where I am, Emma's in danger."

It was a plea for Daniel to get him out of there. Help him to his feet at least.

He'd made some stupid choices, but he would never bring danger to her doorstep. Not if he could help it.

Daniel's face remained hard to read. "Nobody knows you're here. I intend things to stay that way, at least for a few days."

A few days. That was how long Daniel thought it would take to get him on his feet?

He wanted to argue, but what good would it do? Right now he was as weak as a newborn kitten.

"Do you think he can handle some broth?"

Emma's sweet voice rang out from somewhere beyond the doorway. And then the swish of her skirts preceded her as she swept into the room.

"Why don't you ask him?" Daniel's voice was tight when he spoke the words.

"He's—" *Awake?*

She didn't have to finish the question for Seb to know what she'd meant. He'd been able to read her thoughts. She wasn't good at hiding her emotions, her expressive features gave everything away.

But then he remembered how callously she'd rejected him. Maybe it'd all been a lie. Every shy glance, every blush...

Now, she bit her lip. Her gaze fluttered around him like an anxious butterfly afraid to land.

She carried a tray in front of her, a steaming bowl of what must be the broth she'd mentioned.

Her eyes dropped, her lashes hiding her expression, but not before he realized that she wanted to turn around and leave the room.

She didn't.

She didn't look at him again, but she walked right around the couch, going behind Seb's head instead of brushing past Daniel.

Did she do it on purpose, so he couldn't watch her?

She moved into sight and set the tray on the corner of the low table, using one hand to move the glass out of the way before she pushed the tray into place in the center.

Her hands flexed as she straightened. She still wouldn't look at Seb, and some stubborn, prideful part of him used that fact to stare at her, taking in every detail. The peep of dark boots beneath the hem of her skirt. The slender wrists and delicate hands he remembered holding. The single dark-blonde curl that had escaped the twist of hair behind her head. That curl rested just behind her jaw, touching skin that Seb knew firsthand was soft as silk.

"I'll spoon-feed him," Daniel said.

Seb ripped his gaze away from Emma with some effort. Daniel was glaring at him.

Seb glared back. He was half-afraid that Daniel had seen his old feelings, resurrected and bubbling to the surface. He'd loved Emma so deeply that losing her had meant losing a part of himself.

Emma moved toward her brother, giving Seb her profile.

"I can handle it." She probably didn't mean for him to hear her low tone.

"He can barely move," came Daniel's dry reply.

They were talking about him as if he weren't sitting right here. It was humiliating to be reliant on their kindness to eat so he could regain his strength.

He had no intention of letting Emma spoon-feed him.

He would rather die.

He fueled his humiliation into anger, which swept through him long enough to propel himself to a sitting position. His feet fell to the floor as he twisted his body.

The siblings broke off their hushed argument to look his way.

He pressed back into the upper cushions, sweating and clammy, trembling with pain.

"I'll feed my own self, thank you."

Emma clasped her hands at her waist.

Seb's eyes were near crossing from the pain—being upright somehow compressed the injury in his side—but he thought her fingers trembled.

Daniel's gaze narrowed, hard as flint again. He strode to the sofa and handed Seb the bowl of broth. "If you rip out those stitches, the doc'll have to come and put 'em in all over again."

And it was clear that Daniel didn't want that. He wanted Seb gone.

No more than Seb wanted to be gone. He held the other man's stare. "I didn't rip them."

The bowl was warm against his lap.

He wasn't hungry.

But with an older brother for a doctor, he knew he needed to eat if his body was going to repair itself.

Pride forced him to lift the spoon to his lips. The broth was flavorful, and the moment it hit his stomach, his body remembered that he'd been near unconscious for days. He was suddenly ravenous, his stomach demanding more.

He spooned more broth into his mouth, covertly watching Daniel and Emma.

She still hadn't spoken directly to him.

Daniel had his arm under her elbow. He'd guided her away from Seb to the window where she'd stood earlier.

"You don't need to be in here," Daniel said in a low voice.

Too bad Seb had grown up with a bunch of older brothers who'd been trying to keep secrets from him—and each other. His ears were as sharp as an owl's.

"I'm fine," Emma returned. "It doesn't bother me to—to help."

Seb felt his lips curl in a sneer. How magnanimous of her. She no longer wanted him, but she was willing to nurse him.

Daniel shook his head. "You should stay clear of him."

Seb's eyes narrowed. Daniel had been cold since he'd stepped in the room. Did he know more than he'd let on about Seb's activities around town? Why else would he want Emma to stay away?

She was her own woman. She could make her own choices.

Not that Seb had a shred of hope that she'd choose to be with him if she felt she had a choice. She'd up and left the ranch in Wyoming without so much as a word.

He made himself stare at her. This was the woman who'd broken his heart. She was a liar and a tease.

Except the longer his gaze lingered, the more he saw. She wasn't quite looking Daniel in the face either. Oh, her face was tilted up to him, but her eyes weren't focused on her brother.

Her eyes.

His memory provided a blip of the moment she'd set the tray on the table right in front of him. She hadn't looked at the glass before she'd moved it. Her fingertips had dragged along the surface of the table until she'd located it. It'd been quick, but not as quick as using her eyes.

Earlier today, she'd touched Seb's wrist when she'd checked on him. She hadn't spoken to him, even though he'd stared at her rudely.

And right now, she was standing close in conversation with her brother, looking at him without really looking.

Was something wrong with her eyes?

3

Early the next morning, Emma warmed a batch of porridge as Daniel readied for another day in the office.

She hadn't slipped into the parlor to check on Seb. Not yet.

Last night, she'd left when Daniel had insisted he'd help Seb finish what little supper he'd taken.

She was a coward, but she'd been relieved to escape.

Seb had barely spoken—and none of it had been particularly polite—but simply hearing his voice again resurrected memories she'd rather keep buried.

The touch of his hand as they walked side-by-side. The way his breath had felt against her jaw when he'd whispered how much he cared for her.

She'd known having him there would be difficult. But when she'd heard how badly injured he was, she'd wanted him close. Wanted to take care of him.

She also wanted to hide from him.

She was a completely different person now from the girl who'd left Wyoming two years before. She'd had to re-learn how to accomplish daily tasks. She no longer struggled with dressing herself or fixing a meal. She'd learned to do everything that needed to be done.

And she desperately didn't want to be the object of Seb's pity.

She heard Daniel moving around in his room upstairs. He didn't want her near Seb—that was her brother, who'd been overprotective ever since she'd been forced to reveal her feelings for Seb—but she didn't see much choice. Daniel defended the poor and underprivileged in his law practice. He frequently had meetings from sunrise until sundown.

She was going to have to pretend to be okay with waiting on Seb while her brother worked.

Might as well start pretending now.

She straightened her shoulders and turned to the hall. She'd check on Seb first. Prove that Daniel didn't have anything to worry about.

She only faltered once, just outside the parlor door, where she paused to take a shaky breath.

There was a groan and a gasp from inside.

Her hesitation dissipated, and she walked inside.

His groan must mean he was awake. She would hate to wake him if he weren't.

There was a rustling from the sofa as if he'd moved his legs.

"Good morning." There. She kept her voice from shaking. She moved carefully around the sofa.

"No brother on guard duty this morning?"

She should go. Retreat. But his words nudged the tiniest spark of defiance and blew it into a flame. Her chin came up. "I have no need for a guard. We're friends, aren't we?"

He made a noise of derision. "Are we?"

Her stomach dipped like a pail spilling water. She'd known she would hurt him when she'd left. Then, it had felt like a necessity. Now, the anger behind his words simply hurt her.

She pressed her lips together lest he see them tremble. She'd taken a step to retreat to the kitchen—intent on having Daniel bring Seb's breakfast after all—when he spoke again quickly.

"I'm thirsty. The water glass is empty."

She was torn between escaping and retrieving his glass. The Seb she'd once known would have asked politely for more water. This Seb, this stranger, had only demanded.

She'd never been able to ignore an injured animal. Seb's distress was even worse. She remembered how fiercely independent he was. It was probably killing him to be bedridden, to have to depend on her and Daniel for help.

She crossed the room to fetch his glass. She stretched out her hand and swept her fingertips across the surface of the low table. She'd instinctually gone to the end of the

table nearest his head, because surely that was where
Daniel would've left the glass last night, within easy reach
for Seb. But her fingers encountered no glass. The table
was empty.

"It's right over there," he said.

Embarrassment pinked her cheeks. She'd never
wanted him to know about her blindness. She had wanted
his last memories of her to be the strong, independent,
beautiful girl that she'd been in Wyoming.

She swept her hand across the table in more of an arc.

"No, there."

Who could've known that just retrieving a simple glass
from the table would reveal her condition to him?

Her hand finally bumped into the glass at the complete
opposite end of the table. She clasped it in shaking fingers
and straightened. It was empty after all. And how had it
come to be so far out of his reach? And then she remembered his groan from just before she'd entered the room.
Had this been a ruse? A test? The heat in her face became
unbearable at his cruelty, and she turned away.

"Emma."

She could bear his presence no longer and swept out of
the room in such a rush that she misjudged the doorway
and banged her elbow on the frame. Moisture sprang to
her eyes. She hurried back into the kitchen, pretending the
tears were from her smarting elbow and not the encounter
itself.

Her breaths came ragged as she clutched the edge of
the work counter.

Daniel's noises from the second story moved out of his bedroom. Overhead, his footsteps traveled across the hall, which meant she had only a scant few moments to compose herself.

She dashed the evidence from her cheeks and dried her hands on the apron she'd tied around her waist.

She worked to steady her breathing and her hands as she made up a tray for Seb. The porridge would have to do for his breakfast. She refilled his water glass. And then, on second thought, she carefully poured him a cup of coffee from the kettle on the stove.

She added the coffee to the tray as Daniel's familiar footsteps carried him into the room.

"Good morning," she said, mustering as much calm and cheer as she could.

He didn't respond to her greeting immediately, and she had the uncomfortable feeling that he was staring at her. She bore it stoically, though she wanted to run upstairs and throw herself on her bed and cry.

Seb had tricked her. Seb knew the truth—or part of it at least.

She kept her face a serene mask.

"Good morning," Daniel finally said.

"Would you mind taking the tray in to Seb while I dish up your breakfast?"

Daniel didn't acknowledge the slight tremble in her voice. Good. She heard the rattle of the spoon as he lifted the tray and then the murmur of two men's voices in the other room.

She moved mechanically to fill a bowl for Daniel and one for herself—not that she had any appetite.

Her brother returned almost immediately.

She took her bowl to the small table tucked beneath a window at the back of the kitchen. Spring was coming, or so everyone said. But all she felt was a cool draft coming in through the casement.

Daniel remained at the counter. He often ate standing up in the mornings, eager to get to the office.

Indeed, his voice was garbled as he spoke with his mouth half full. "You look a little peaked. You sure you're all right if I go into the office?"

She worked to keep her expression peaceful. "Why should today be any different? Seb has been under our roof for days already."

"But today he's awake."

Her smile slipped, and she quickly spooned some of the porridge into her mouth. After she'd eaten the bite, she answered. "It will be fine."

No, it wouldn't. But she wouldn't ask Daniel to stay home to baby her. Nor would she turn away Edgar's brother when he was in such desperate health. She and her older sister Fran had suffered a series of misfortunes, and when a vile lunatic had chased Emma across the country, Fran had protected her. Ultimately, the sisters had ended up in Wyoming, and Fran had been caught in a sticky situation and ended up married to Edgar.

Edgar and his brothers had protected the both of them.

In the midst of it all, Fran had fallen for Edgar. They remained happily married.

Emma would never forget what she owed her brother-in-law. Her life, and her sister's.

Taking care of Seb, as uncomfortable as it would be, was the least she could do.

"And if he discovers you're blind?"

It was what she'd been most afraid of two years ago when an illness and high fever had robbed her of her sight.

She'd been forced to confess her feelings to Daniel. Daniel knew she'd loved Seb—but not that her feelings had never faded.

Her lips trembled now. "I'm fairly certain he's already figured it out." Before Daniel could play the protective older brother, she rushed on. "Phillip is coming by later to help with my manuscript. I'll be too busy to worry." A lie. "I'll check on Seb a few times. Everything will be fine." Another lie.

Daniel hesitated. "You're sure?"

She released the breath she'd been holding. He believed her. "Of course."

She heard the clink of his bowl as he placed it on the counter. Daniel's mind had no doubt gone to his caseload, the people he'd see today.

But he paused at the door. "It would be best if you didn't mention any of this to Phillip. Seb. Or his condition."

"Why?"

She felt the waves of tension roll off Daniel at her inno-cent question.

"You refused to tell me how Seb was injured." She wasn't sure her brother even knew. The fact that Seb had been dropped on their doorstep in the middle of the night was suspicious, wasn't it? "And now you want me to keep him a secret? What's going on?"

"Nothing you need to concern yourself over. Just do as I say."

There he went again, ordering her around. Two years they'd lived together. Seemed by now he'd have learned she didn't take his orders.

She wanted to argue, but her brother left the room.

She bit back a sound of frustration.

Daniel had helped her in so many ways after she'd lost her sight. But lately, his protectiveness rankled.

Didn't she deserve to know why Seb had been so griev-ously injured?

Of course, she could always ask the man himself.

If she asked Seb questions, then he'd question her as well.

And she wasn't quite sure she could bear that.

SEB HEARD Emma and Daniel's voices in the kitchen and then footsteps—Daniel's heavier tread and sure stride—go back down the hall and then leave out the front door.

He picked at the porridge as he waited for Emma to

return. He hated porridge, but his body demanded sustenance.

Emma was blind.

He'd suspected as much. He'd baited his trap. And he'd received his answer as he'd watched her sweep her hand across the table to locate his empty glass.

Emma was blind, and her condition prompted many questions.

How long ago had it happened? She moved with easy grace around the home she shared with Daniel, as if she'd had lots of time to get used to the home. She'd been the one to provide Seb with broth, and he suspected, the porridge. Which meant she was comfortable enough in the kitchen to cook. Which supported his theory that she'd had a lot of time to practice.

Was it difficult for her to manage in her condition?

The thought fueled the fire of his temper. Emma didn't deserve compassion from him. She'd walked away without looking back. Torn his heart to shreds when she'd done so.

Emma didn't care about him.

And he didn't want to care about her.

She's taking care of you now, whispered an insidious voice in his head.

Because she had no other choice. He still didn't know how he'd ended up here, in Daniel's house. But he knew Emma had a bleeding heart, and she wouldn't put him out as long as he was injured.

That didn't mean she held any tender feelings for him.

He had a long time to be caught in the vortex of his swirling thoughts before she returned.

He'd set aside the half-empty bowl of porridge and reclined on the sofa, this time with his uninjured arm thrown across his eyes.

Maybe he'd dozed off, or maybe she'd tiptoed into the room, but the soft clink of the spoon against the bowl made him twitch. He moved his arm to his side, the movement too quick and jerky, and he couldn't help the grunt of pain, though he attempted to bite it off.

"Sorry to disturb you," she said in a cool, no-nonsense tone. "I didn't know if you were awake."

It's your home. The words he should speak caught in his throat. *And I am at your mercy.* But his confusing feelings kept the words behind his clenched teeth.

She settled his bowl and glass in the center of the tray, her movements as graceful as ever.

"Why didn't you tell me?" He hadn't meant the words to emerge at all, never mind how petulant his voice sounded.

When she straightened, the way she clutched the tray between them made him think of a knight's shield from a story. "You were unconscious until late yesterday."

That wasn't what he meant and she knew it.

"Does Fran know?"

This question was met with a tight nod.

Fran knew, which meant Seb's brother Edgar knew as well. The couple kept no secrets from each other.

But they'd kept this from Seb. And probably from the

rest of the family. His large, crazy family was close, which made it almost impossible to keep secrets.

And suddenly, Seb experienced a visceral memory of his brother Maxwell—a doctor—avoiding him at the last family supper Seb had been to. Suspicion rose, choking him. Had Maxwell known?

"When did it happen?" he demanded, as if he had a right to know.

Twin spots of color rose in her fair cheeks. "It doesn't matter."

Of course, it mattered.

He pushed himself up on his elbow, the action making his breath ragged. He hated being flat on his back, hated being weak.

"Tell me."

She could've left the room, but she didn't. Her gaze was fixed somewhere above his head. He saw the shift of her feet, knew he was making her uncomfortable.

And maybe it was callous of him, but he couldn't find it in himself to care.

He deserved to know.

"I lost my sight from that fever I took. Just before I left h—Wyoming." Her hands were shaking, rattling the dishes on the tray.

He'd thought he wanted to know, but the confirmation that his suspicions were right was like a blow to his abused ribs.

"And if you hadn't nearly gotten yourself killed, you

would never have known." The words seemed ripped from her lips.

She turned and started for the door.

He fell back on the sofa, his strength gone.

She hadn't wanted him to know.

Because he hadn't been good enough for her.

She'd somehow seen what he'd spent years trying to overcome.

And she'd cut ties.

He was torn from his thoughts by a firm knock on the front door. Emma had retreated to the kitchen.

His anger and hurt were immediately forgotten, stuffed away to be dealt with later.

Someone was at the door. It might be one of Tolliver's thugs.

He almost called out to her to tell her not to answer the door. But his voice would alert whoever was at the door to his presence.

He might deserve the beating he'd received, but the last thing he wanted was Emma caught up with the dangerous criminals who were looking for him.

He couldn't let her get hurt because of him.

EMMA PRESSED her clammy hands to her cheeks, trying to slow the storm of her breathing.

Since the moment five days ago when her brother had revealed it was Seb fighting for his life in their parlor, she'd known this confrontation was inevitable.

She'd hoped to avoid it. Tried to put her thoughts in some semblance of order so she could explain things adequately to him.

But she hadn't been ready.

Someone was knocking at the door.

That was Phillip. And she was so flustered and upset by Seb's sharp words that she was very near tears.

Phillip knocked again, and she took a deep breath, striving to pull herself together. She moved down the front hall to the door. Her hands were still trembling as she reached for the latch.

"Good morning, Emma." Phillip was unfailingly polite, as usual.

"Good morning." Could he see the emotion on her face?

From the parlor, she heard a thump. She had no desire for Phillip to know about Seb's presence. It didn't matter that Daniel had asked her to keep Seb a secret. Right now, she couldn't answer a single question about the man she'd once loved. She wasn't even sure whether she'd be able to force her mind to focus on the manuscript she and Phillip were working on.

Another thump, this one quite close to the parlor door. What was that man doing?

She ushered Phillip quickly through the hall, hoping he hadn't noticed anything amiss. "Why don't you go ahead and set up at the kitchen table? I'll be right there to pour you a cup of coffee. I forgot ... something ... in the other room."

She could only hope that Phillip complied as she rushed back to the parlor. She opened the door and quickly closed it behind her. She was turning when her senses registered the tall presence too close. She could feel the heat radiating from him, smell the sharp scent of medicine still on his breath.

She stepped back. "What are you doing?" she hissed.

"Who was at the door?" His voice was a faint rasp, and each breath came fast and shallow.

There was no way she was telling him anything about Phillip. She needed to get him back on the sofa. What on earth had possessed him to get up? Had he injured himself further?

"You shouldn't be up." She reached out her hand without thinking it through. Her palm connected with the soft flannel undershirt Daniel had put him in. Beneath the shirt's softness, the muscles in his side tensed, and for one moment she thought she'd inadvertently pressed against his injury. But he stayed tense, muscles coiled. She felt him gasping for breath.

"I shouldn't be up."

"That's what I said—"

He slumped, his shoulder settling against the wall. He was upright, but maybe not for long.

She slid her arm around his side, nudging her shoulder up into his armpit. He was so big. She remembered him being taller than she was, but this bulk... He had filled out in the two years since she'd been away. And from what she could feel, it was all muscle.

"Who's at the door?" he slurred. "Gotta... make sure..." He mumbled something else, his voice is too low for her to understand. She thought it sounded like *in danger*.

Why would there be danger? She hadn't realized she'd spoken in the words aloud until he mumbled, "... gotta be sure you're safe." His words were hot against the top of her head.

He thought she was in danger, and that's why he'd gotten out of bed?

"Foolish man," she murmured. "It was just a friend."

She was afraid that he was going to topple right over, and if he did, she wouldn't be able to drag him back to the sofa herself. Daniel didn't want Phillip to know Seb was here. Which meant she needed to maneuver Seb back onto the sofa before he collapsed.

"Can you walk?"

Seb only grunted as she urged him the first few steps back across the room. He leaned heavily on her shoulder, his steps dragging.

"Foolish man," she said under her breath.

"I don't... remember you... talking to me like that before."

She barely resisted the urge to punch him in the side. "I don't remember you ever giving me a reason to," she countered.

Her thigh brushed the arm of the sofa, just like she'd expected, and she stepped out from under his arm, placing his hand on the armrest.

"Can you manage?" she asked.

A grunt was all she got in response, but she heard the sound of him settling into the cushions, not a thump on the floor.

Phillip was waiting, so she forced herself to walk away. "I'll be back in a while to check on you."

It wasn't until she was out in the hall, closing the door, that she realized he hadn't tried to direct her across the room. He'd trusted her to get him back to the sofa even without her sight. Had it only been because he was in so much pain that he'd forgotten about her condition?

She went into the kitchen and turned toward the stove, where the coffeepot waited. She sensed Phillip in the corner where he usually sat across from her at the little table.

"I already poured," he said. "Yours is here at the table."

She felt her irritation rise but worked to squash it. She and Phillip had worked together for months. He probably hadn't given any thought to pouring the coffee. They were friends. Maybe he felt at home to serve himself, even if she hadn't given him leave to do it.

When she settled at the second chair at the table and smoothed her skirt over her legs, she still felt flustered.

"Is everything all right?" he asked.

She tried to find a smile, tried to forget that Seb was in the next room, that he thought there was danger.

Phillip was here to work.

"Yes, sorry. Just a little distracted today." She could only pray that he wouldn't ask more. "Would you mind reading a few lines from where we stopped last week?"

It was part of their routine, hearing what she imagined and he'd typed from the last session would engage her memory and hopefully help her focus.

She took a sip of coffee and returned the mug to the table. She clasped her hands loosely on top of the table.

Without warning, one of Phillip's warm hands closed over hers.

She jumped, and he let go.

"Sorry." He exhaled noisily. "There's something I want to talk about before we get started for the day."

Still reeling from the unexpected touch, she sat silently. What could he possibly have to talk to her about?

"I submitted your first manuscript to a publisher."

His words were so unexpected that it took a moment for her to process them. When she did, it was with a sharp gasp. "What? Why would you do that?"

"Why would you write the book if you didn't want it to be published someday?" He sounded genuinely perplexed, but that didn't stop her from snapping at him.

"*Someday*. That book wasn't ready for someone else to look at it."

She sensed movement, but there was no sound. Maybe he'd shaken his head?

"Your ability to tell a story is incredible. You don't give yourself enough credit."

His words made her blush, but they still didn't change things.

"You still shouldn't have done it. It was my book—"

"I didn't steal it, if that's what you're thinking. I sent everything with your name attached to it."

That wasn't the point.

"I'm sorry you're upset, but it's done now. If they reject it, you can have the manuscript back and lock it in a drawer or whatever you want. But if they decide to publish it..."

She shook her head. She's written a book because she'd wanted to. She had a wild hope that maybe someday —in the far future—she would have the courage to submit it to a publisher. But it wasn't ready yet. They wouldn't want her book.

"Look, I'm sorry."

Though he didn't sound it, and it wasn't much of an apology. Part of her was furious that Phillip had taken the liberty to do such a thing. Part of her was excited in a nervous way.

There was no changing what he'd done. No way to get the manuscript back until the publisher returned it. And after that, she would make sure that Phillip didn't have a chance to *help* her again.

4
———

It was midafternoon before Seb saw Emma again. She backed into the room and then turned, revealing that she held a tray again. He hated that she was forced to take care of him like this.

He stifled a groan as he pushed himself into a seated position.

"Did you rip your stitches during your foolish heroic act earlier?"

Some greeting. He grimaced as her words conjured the memory of being so weak he could barely stand. He'd embarrassed himself for sure.

"I'm fine." Earlier, he'd lifted the borrowed nightshirt to check his bandages. No blood seeped through the one on his side. He didn't think he'd done additional damage.

She moved toward him, each step graceful and sure.

"Please tell me there's a plate full of roast and potatoes for me. I can't take any more porridge or broth." He'd been smelling the savory scents all afternoon, and his stomach was rumbling. It was pure torture.

She didn't smile. "You'll have what I serve you and that's that."

But when she placed the tray on the low table, he was gratified to see heaping portions of roast and potatoes and carrots. "You're a good friend."

As he watched, some emotion crossed her face before she hid it behind a placid expression. "Am I now?"

He probably owed her an apology for how he'd acted that morning. It wasn't until he'd heard her friend knock that he'd realized just how precarious a position his presence had put Emma in. If Tolliver got a whiff of the fact that Seb was there, that he was alive, he'd send someone to finish Seb off. And he wouldn't let anyone stand in the way.

It no longer mattered that Emma had left him. Or that she hadn't trusted him with the truth about her condition. He'd stuffed his anger down deep inside where it couldn't see the light of day.

The only thing that remained was his fierce need to protect her. He might have walked away from his family, gotten wrapped up in some ugly dealings with Tolliver, done things he wasn't proud of. But he refused to let Emma get hurt.

He was going to get back on his feet as fast as he could. And get out of there.

She turned her head slightly as if thinking of heading for the door.

"Would you sit with me for a bit?" He picked up the plate and fork. Maybe the potatoes weren't as perfectly cubed as they might've been if a sighted person had made the meal, but otherwise there was no way to tell that it had been made by someone who couldn't see. This close, the aroma had his mouth watering. "I don't know how much longer I can take the boredom of being alone in here."

He did win a smile at that, although a small one. And when she perched on the edge of a tall-backed chair nearby, he felt like he had won.

He shoveled a forkful of roast into his mouth and groaned.

She straightened, one hand pressing against the arm of the chair, ready to jump to his aid. "What's wrong? Are you in pain?"

"Iff's delicious." His ma would tan his hide if she'd heard him speak with his mouth full like that. He didn't care. He was in heaven. He hadn't eaten a home-cooked meal like this in ages.

Emma relaxed into the chair.

He swallowed and inhaled another bite before he said, "In the spirit of friendship, I've got to ask. Does your brother know about your beau?"

She shook her head, her expression puzzled.

"The man you just spent three hours with."

He might've stuffed the confusing tangle of his feelings about Emma way down deep, but for a moment, he was glad that she couldn't see his expression, just in case he hadn't been able to wipe away all of the jealousy her visitor had inspired. He had no right to it. He knew it was wrong. But that hadn't stopped the ugly feeling from ripping his insides to shreds all morning.

"That wasn't ... anyone special." The fact that she stumbled over her words told him more than she probably wanted him to know. "Phillip and I work together."

Phillip. He had a name, but Seb hadn't gotten a glimpse of her man.

"What kind of work?" Maybe his skepticism had been audible in his voice, because she shot him a look that his sister Brianna would've been proud of. One that told him that whatever had happened in the kitchen today wasn't any of his business.

"Never mind," he said. "What you and your sweetheart do is none of my business."

She opened her mouth as if readying herself to tell him off, then closed it again.

He shoveled in a few more bites, clearing his plate in a way that would've made his brothers back home proud. He was one of six boys who'd found their way to Jonas White as the man had moved west from Philadelphia with his infant daughter, Breanna. Seb had been young—four, maybe—when Jonas had found him on the street in a small western town that Seb wasn't even sure had a name. He'd been starving and alone, and with no one to claim him, Jonas had taken him in. Each of Seb's older brothers had found a home with Jonas in a different way. Matty's family had died of a fever. Edgar had come west on an orphan train. Maxwell had been abused. Penny, Jonas's wife, had come into their lives later. She was a saint to have taken on a ready-made family made up of seven orphan boys and a precocious little girl. Or maybe she'd just loved Pa that much.

Emma surprised him out of his thoughts with a question. "Are you going to tell me why you think danger is following you around?"

He nearly choked on the bite in his mouth.

She must've heard, because she wore a smug little smile. Whatever twisted enjoyment he had gotten from needling her moments ago evaporated.

"How did I end up here? In your house?" he asked.

"I'm not entirely sure. It was the middle of the night. I woke up disoriented. When I came downstairs, Daniel was there and so were you, half-dead."

Seb remembered her brother's glare from this morning. Daniel knew more than he was letting on. Seb needed to talk to him.

His appetite satisfied, he set the plate down and reclined against the cushions.

He relaxed his neck, his head tipping back slightly, but he didn't stop looking at her. He'd leave as soon as he was able—a few days at the most—and right now he wanted nothing more than to fill his memory with the most beautiful woman he'd ever seen.

"If the men who tried to kill me find out I'm still alive, they'll return to finish the job."

Emma flinched. "Why do they want to kill you?"

No way was he regaling her with the sordid history of

how he'd ended up in Tolliver's employ. He'd made his choices, and he'd live with them. Emma didn't need to know that he was an enforcer who'd had a sudden change of heart. "I know some things I'm not supposed to know." That was technically true.

He saw the minute tension leave her shoulders. "In that case, should I ask a deputy to come round? Surely they can find who did this to you."

"No." His vehemence seemed to startle her. "That won't help," he went on more slowly.

He knew the local sheriff had tried to take down Tolliver before. Clean up his city, as it were. But nothing had stuck, and Tolliver had retaliated by killing a sheriff's deputy—a crime that had never been pinned on him, either.

Seb had plenty of dirt on Tolliver, but if he got the law involved, he would end up implicating himself. Seb was the one who'd beat a man to within an inch of his life for not paying Tolliver's protection fee. He was the one who'd threatened dozens of families. Stood by and looked the other way when Tolliver's men broke into the storefront belonging to a man who wouldn't pay up.

If Seb went to the sheriff, he would end up in prison for sure.

Thinking of all he'd done, he felt dirty just sitting across from Emma.

"As soon as I can move around a little better, I'll be out of your hair."

Some emotion he couldn't read crossed her face.

"But until then, it's better if no one knows I'm here. You should keep to your regular routines as much as possible."

"Daniel suggested I shouldn't leave the house," she murmured. "Though he didn't say it outright."

Did Daniel suspect someone was watching?

All of a sudden, he was exhausted. His eyes became too heavy to hold open.

He needed to talk to Daniel. Maybe if he rested now, he could see the other man when he returned home.

He wished for a couple of his brothers. If Edgar and Matty were here, they'd keep watch. Keep Emma safe.

Because right this moment, he was weaker than a baby.

"Lie back down." At the soft touch of Emma's hands at his shoulder, he had to stifle a whimper. No matter that he was still angry at her, no matter that he was putting her in danger... he wanted her to touch his face. Wanted her to touch her lips to his.

A hysterical cackle was barely contained by gritting his teeth together.

He'd kissed *her* before, but the shy Emma he'd known would never initiate a kiss.

His wild thoughts had to have been coming from the pain coursing through his body. His brain trying to distract him.

He allowed her to help him get flat on his back again—hating every moment—and then before he could even murmur a thank you, he was unconscious again.

5

Emma was preparing for bed when Daniel knocked on her door. She had her hair down and was brushing the long strands to smoothness as she bade him enter.

"I've got another hour of reading to do," her brother said. "I thought I'd better say good-night now."

No one worked harder than Daniel. He defended unfortunate souls who needed help, like the young man who had been injured by factory machinery so badly that he'd lost his hand and remained unable to work. The company had let him go without a penny. Daniel had fought—and won—a settlement for him.

Her brother often worked long into the night. He was passionate about his cases, even when the people he helped couldn't pay him. His caseload never seemed to decrease. There was always someone who needed help.

As of late, before Seb had dropped onto their doorstep, Emma had found herself lonelier than ever.

Sometimes she ached for the bustle of the homestead-turned-ranch that belonged to Seb's father and brothers. There was always work to be done, but more than that, there was always someone around. Penny, in the big main kitchen, cooking up grub for her large family. One of the men breaking a horse in the corral. Before Emma had left, she'd been close with Breanna, who had married and moved away from home, and Velma, the young daughter of Seb's brother Oscar.

And of course, her sister Fran was there. Fran and Edgar had increased their family by a daughter. A baby—toddler now—that Emma had never had a chance to cuddle. And Fran was in the family way again.

Emma ached to see her sister and her niece.

She hated to mention her loneliness to Daniel. When she'd lost her sight, he'd been the one to uproot the life he was building in Wyoming and move to Denver. She'd only wanted to escape the White's family homestead. Daniel had believed he'd be able to build a clientele here and he'd been right.

He'd worked hard to make a good life for both of them.

So instead of mentioning her loneliness, she'd told him that she'd always wanted to write a book, and Daniel had found her a typist. Phillip.

But having Seb underfoot today had brought back her desire to go back to Wyoming.

"Seb told me he might be in danger," she said.

Daniel's constant movement stopped suddenly. Her brother had gone very still. "That's nothing for you to worry about. He'll be gone in a few days."

"Do you think so? He stood up and hobbled across the room when Phillip came, and it took him all afternoon to recover."

Her brother grumbled under his breath. "He'd better be."

She hated to think about someone stalking Seb. She still remembered the terror of those days when Underhill —a lunatic who fancied himself in love with her—had chased her and Fran across the country. And nearly caught them. Fran had been injured and horsewhipped.

Emma had been terrified. It had taken months for her nightmares to recede.

"I wouldn't have him here if I thought it put you in danger," Daniel said.

She knew that. She wasn't worried about herself, only Seb. He was so weak. How could he defend himself if he needed to?

The idea had been circling in her head all afternoon and evening. Surely there was a way for both of them to solve both of their problems.

"What if I escorted Seb home to Wyoming?" she asked, her voice more tentative than she would've liked.

"Out of the question," Daniel said immediately.

"Whatever feelings there once were between us are gone." At least on his side. She shrugged. "We're like family now, like brother and sister."

She couldn't see Daniel's expression, obviously, but she could almost feel waves of skepticism rolling off of him.

"He was very angry with me this morning." Surely Seb's anger meant whatever tender feelings he once had were gone. He would never have acted so poorly toward her when they'd courted.

Daniel's footsteps let her know he was coming near. When he reached out and gently patted her shoulder, it was instinct to hide her surprise. His touches were sporadic and she never knew when they were coming. Now it seemed he wanted to offer comfort.

"Did he say something untoward? I can speak to him."

"That's not necessary. We've made our peace." It was a tenuous peace to be certain. She still wasn't sure why Seb had been more kind in the afternoon. Tension remained between them, but it hadn't been as toothy as it had been in the morning.

"Regardless of any impropriety," Daniel said, "Seb is greatly injured, and I'm not certain he could look after you on a long train journey."

"I can look after myself."

She placed the hairbrush on her bed and turned so that she faced him more fully, or at least she hoped so.

"I go to the butcher's and baker's every Wednesday," she reminded him.

"It's not the same." He spoke the words gently, but it didn't stop them from slicing into Emma.

"I'm right in the middle of this big case with Elbert. If I

weren't, I could take you for a visit to Fran, if that's what you want."

She couldn't help but notice he didn't mention Seb.

"A journey like that, on your own... Emma, you must understand that I only want what's best for you."

He spoke the words with a finality that let her know, in his mind, the matter was closed. Part of her wanted to argue, to lay out all of the ways she'd grown in the past two years, the things she was capable of now. But another part of her spirit shrank and shriveled. Maybe Daniel was right. She'd grown confident in moving about her daily life, but boarding a train full of strangers, possibly having to change trains, finding food to eat, and also taking care of her own necessary functions... It did seem daunting.

"I know you have a lot of work waiting for you," she said. "I'll say good-night."

Daniel stood there another moment, and she could feel his gaze. Did he know the smile she'd donned was false? As children, they hadn't been close, as she was nine years his junior, but losing her sight had changed everything. Daniel had taken care of her through those first long, dark days. He'd encouraged her when her spirits were so low that she hadn't wanted to get out of bed. She knew he loved her and only wanted good for her.

But when he left her to finish getting ready for bed, the chasm of loneliness opened up inside her.

Would it ever go away?

·   ·   ·

THE NEXT MORNING, Seb woke to find Daniel sitting in the chair across from him, staring at him. It was early, the sun just beginning to lighten the sky outside the windows behind Emma's brother.

"What's the matter?" Seb asked.

"I don't want you under my roof any more than you want to be here," the other man said. "I took you in as a favor to your family. Your brothers rescued Fran and Emma when I couldn't be there for them. I figure this makes us even. But I won't tolerate cruelty toward Emma."

There it was. Yesterday, Emma'd claimed that Daniel wasn't her guard dog, but she must've mentioned their angry exchange or Daniel wouldn't be here now.

Daniel had always been something of a beanpole, and Seb had always thought of him as bookish. He wasn't a man who worked with his hands, and it showed. But right now, the stiff way he held himself and the protective light in his eyes showed Seb he meant business. Good. Emma needed someone to look after her.

"Understood." He had no intention of crossing swords with Emma again. But he was glad Daniel had come to him. They needed to talk. "How exactly did I end up on your doorstep?"

Daniel's eyes narrowed. "I work with clients all across the city. From all different backgrounds and in all different jobs. People talk to me. I heard about it when you came to town." He left unsaid that he also knew what Seb had been up to, though Seb didn't doubt it. "I probably should've wired your pa to tell him to come and get you."

Seb shoved himself up on his elbow, regretting the action immediately as pain clawed through his innards. "I'm my own man. I don't need Pa to come to fetch me out of trouble like a schoolboy."

Pa would be ashamed if he knew what Seb had been doing.

"The decisions you've made haven't shown a hint of maturity."

Seb scowled.

"I asked a couple of trustworthy fellas to keep an ear open for any news of you getting in trouble. One of them found you in the street, bleeding out. And he brought you here, thinking I'd want to help you."

Shoot. That was not good. No matter how trustworthy Daniel thought his man was, he knew where Seb was and likely who he worked for. If he told a single soul, word could spread. Or, if Tolliver found out, he could beat Seb's location out of Daniel's man.

"It puts Emma in danger for me to be here."

Daniel nodded grimly. "You got any other friends in the city who'd take you in?"

They both knew that the only kind of friends Seb had made while he'd been in Denver were the kind who'd sell him out for the right price.

"I thought about putting you up in a boarding house, but who'd wait on you? You can't even get up. The doctor said it might take weeks for you to heal."

Daniel wasn't stupid. He didn't like it any better than Seb. But it seemed like he was stuck here, at least for the time being.

Daniel stood. "I'll bring your breakfast when it's ready."

It couldn't be more obvious. He didn't want Emma hanging around Seb any more than she needed to.

It was no more than Seb deserved, but he was still scowling when Daniel left the room.

LATER THAT MORNING, his sausage and eggs long gone, Emma came in carrying a bowl in one hand. She had something tucked in the fold of her apron as she approached.

"Are you still sitting upright?" she asked.

He was, in fact. Trying to build up his tolerance for the low-grade pain in his ribs and side. "Yes, ma'am. What've you got there?"

She edged her way around the low table and placed the bowl on the sofa beside his knee. He saw another, smaller bowl inside the first. She carefully set the bowls side-by-side, making sure the one closest to the edge wasn't going to fall off the sofa.

When she sat on the opposite side of the bowl, he saw the pods of unshelled peas she'd carried in her apron.

"I thought I'd help alleviate your boredom," she said. "Hold out your hands."

He twisted slowly, and even that careful movement pained his ribs. He held his breath against the groan that wanted to escape.

She scooped up two fistfuls of the pods and held them out to him. She misjudged how close they were with the bowl between them, and her wrist bumped his hand.

He adjusted, moving his cupped hands below her closed ones. Maybe he *was* a cruel person, like Daniel said, because he didn't resist the urge to touch his fingertips against the soft skin of her wrist.

A catch in her breath was the only sound in the room. He was a cad above all cads to surprise her with a touch like that, but when else was he going to be close to her? He didn't have the right, but he'd taken the touch anyway.

"Besides," she said as if nothing had happened, "you eat twice as much as Daniel, so you might as well help since you being here makes more work for me."

"You're right." He dropped the pods in his lap and began shelling. One bowl for the peas, one for the pods.

When Emma relaxed into the seat next to him, a feeling he wasn't used to bubbled up beneath his ribs. Peace, maybe? It'd been too long since he hadn't needed to guard his back, since he could just be.

"There are too many peas here for the three of us." His fingers fell into the rhythm of shelling as if he were still the young boy helping Penny and Breanna in the kitchen. Maybe he'd shelled too many peas in his childhood to forget how.

"My garden is overflowing with peas this year," she said. "There's a family down the street that Daniel and I share our bounty with occasionally. Caroline lost her husband two years ago, and she has three young children."

A tragedy, to be sure. But now the woman had Emma looking after her.

"That's a relief. I wasn't looking forward to eating peas for breakfast, lunch, and supper."

She made a little noise that meant she wasn't impressed by his humor.

But he let his fingers keep working and turned his head to look at her. A handful of peas *tinked* into the bowl as his gaze swept over her face. Her hair was pulled back into a twist at the nape of her neck, but fine strands curled at her temple and forehead. Her lashes hid her eyes from him. Her head was angled slightly toward him. Though she wasn't looking at him, it seemed her attention was on him.

He was surprised by the urge that rose up inside and almost strangled him. He wanted to reach out and cup her jaw. Craved the connection. Wanted her to turn toward him, forget about the chore, and fall into his embrace.

The wanting shook him to the core.

She wasn't his. She never had been, not really, even though they'd made promises to each other a long time ago.

But still, there was that anger, hot and boiling, like a hot spring beneath the surface, buried deep inside.

How could he be so angry with her and still want to embrace her?

She seemed unaware of his inner turmoil.

"I was hoping you'd have some recent news from home. Fran writes so sporadically... and of course, your mother is a busy woman. I hate to pester her with correspondence too often."

Her words had tension coiling through him and knocked the air right out of his body.

"I haven't written or heard from anybody since I left," he said tightly.

She frowned. "How long ago?"

"Eighteen months."

She didn't bother hiding her surprise and dismay. "Seb White, your mother must be worried sick!"

His fingers folded over the last of the pea pods in his lap. He shelled them quickly and then let his head flop against the sofa back.

Emma, too, finished her last pod. She scooted to the edge of the cushion, preparing to stand.

"I'll bring you some paper and a pencil. You can write to her now."

"I'm not going to write home," he said.

Emma froze, half-turned toward him. "Why not?"

Because his parents would be shamed to know what he'd been doing, how he'd been making his living. He figured they were better off not knowing, maybe thinking he was dead, than knowing he was a criminal.

Emma's hand rested on his knee, making him flinch at the unexpected contact. "Did you—was there a falling out?"

"I left on good terms." Neither Jonas nor Penny had understood why he'd needed to go. They'd asked him to stay. Penny had shed tears.

But he couldn't stay. Everything about the ranch had chafed after Emma's desertion. Chores that had given him a sense of pride became meaningless. The plans he'd had for a cabin of his own had turned into ash. He'd dreamed of building a life there with Emma, and without her, he couldn't stand any of it.

In the end, his parents had let him go.

"Why did you leave?" she asked.

There was no way he was going to admit to her just how heartbroken he'd been. His weakness made him feel like a fool. And she'd left him behind, gone on with her life. She seemed happy.

His heartbreak was for himself alone.

"Leave it alone, Emma," he said quietly.

He didn't know how she did it when she couldn't see him, but she gave him such a searching look that he opened his mouth to promise he'd write the letter.

But then she stood up, turning away, and the moment was broken.

Good thing, because any promise like that would've been a lie.

He'd dug his own grave by working for Tolliver. He was going to have to find a way to escape. On his own.

6

Two days later, Emma was walking home from visiting her friend Caroline. When she'd delivered the peas and some carrots from her garden two days ago, Caroline's infant son had been battling croup. Emma had never heard such a cough—a sound like a barking dog. She'd heard Caroline's exhaustion in her voice. The woman was a widow and had no family to speak of. Yesterday, Emma had brought her a pot of soup. Today it had been a hearty stew. When Caroline had let Emma in the door, she'd been so overcome that she'd burst into tears.

Emma had ended up staying for the entire afternoon. She'd rocked the baby and told stories to Caroline's toddlers, a girl and a boy, while her friend had gotten some much-needed rest.

Now she walked quickly, the brisk air telling her that

evening was coming on quickly. Daniel had mentioned that he would be working late tonight, but she'd told Seb she was going out for a short while. What if he'd needed something while she was away? She hurried her steps.

Thoughts of Seb weren't the only thing that had her rushing. An uncomfortable feeling was raising tiny hairs at the base of her scalp. As if she was being watched. She'd felt it yesterday, too.

She was probably imagining it. Since the loss of her sight, she sometimes had the feeling that a customer at the mercantile or the bakery was staring at her, though she couldn't be sure without asking somebody.

She held her breath and strained her ears to listen. The Smith family was having a boisterous supper. She could hear the children's chatter from here. A dog was barking, the sound far away. Birds chirped in the big maple on the corner. Those and her footsteps and the tap of her walking stick on the ground were the only sounds she heard. She was the only one on the street right now.

She forced her thoughts from imagined fears. There had to be something else she could do for Caroline. She couldn't imagine the hardships the widow faced, eking out a living and raising three children on her own.

For a moment, Emma thought about her brother's words from days ago. *A journey like that, on your own...*

The memory came to her sometimes in quiet moments. The more she'd thought about Daniel's words, the more she disagreed.

She was capable enough to travel to Wyoming by train. Or to Philadelphia to visit Breanna. She wasn't afraid to ask for help if she needed it.

But she hadn't yet gathered the courage to bring it up to Daniel again. Her brother had been quiet, almost terse with her over the past few days. No doubt he was worried about her being under the same roof as Seb. He needn't worry. She wasn't the same frightened girl she'd been when she'd run from Wyoming, and Seb wasn't the same either. He was harder, somehow. He kept his own counsel, not opening himself to her as he once had.

Whatever love had been between them, it had been a young love, and when she'd left, it had died.

She went up the steps and let herself into the house, settling her cane in the corner out of the way.

Something moved behind her, large and close.

She shrieked and whirled, throwing her hands up in front of her.

"Easy!" Seb's scent registered before his voice did.

He was close. His big hands clasped her wrists. Her heart was beating like a hummingbird's wings trapped behind her breastbone.

Her panic swung wildly into something else, and she gripped his shirt in her fists. She couldn't seem to catch her breath.

And then he was folding her into his arms. His strength was as familiar to her even though he felt so very different, layered with muscles as he was. Her nose pressed into the hot skin just above his collar, her cheek into the softness of his shirt. His hands settled at her waist, hot even through her dress, like twin brands.

"You're trembling," he said, the words warm against the crown of her head. "I didn't mean to frighten you."

"I was only startled. You don't frighten me." She could never be scared, not of him. Being close to him like this settled her. She breathed in and out. "What are you doing off the sofa?"

"You were gone a long time. And somebody knocked earlier. I didn't answer it."

Beneath her cheek, she could hear his heart pounding.

"I got worried."

And with Daniel's words in her ears, her own emerged snappish. "I'm perfectly capable of walking down the street and back."

She felt him shake his head by the movement of his chin. "That's not it at all."

She should step back. This closeness was confusing her. Seb's pounding heart and the frantic rhythm of his breath—as if he cared about what happened to her—played tricks on her mind.

She raised her head from his chest, intending to step back, but he lifted one hand and cupped her cheek.

"Emma, I..." He pressed closer.

She felt the warmth of his breath against her chin, the only warning she had before his lips claimed hers.

This wasn't a chaste kiss like the ones he'd given her in those few weeks they'd had together.

This was a kiss borne of worry, desperation, maybe even anger. Seb's lips slanted over hers, and all she could do was cling to his broad shoulders. Hold on to the man she'd never stopped loving.

She met his kiss like a woman who'd been starved of the one thing she craved the most.

As if he'd realized she was pressing closer, not pulling away, his kiss changed. His hand moved from her cheek to her neck, his thumb brushing her jaw. His mouth softened, became teasing.

And then his kiss was gone. He brushed her lips with his once more, a sweet touch that almost felt like an apology.

She was breathing as fast as if she'd run up the street instead of walking.

He put several inches between them, his hands falling away. Her hands fell to his waist. She wasn't ready to let go of him or this moment. Not yet.

"We shouldn't have done that." His voice was rough and low. "Your brother won't appreciate me taking advantage."

He said the words. But she wasn't sure she believed him. Not when he could easily step away from her touch.

"You didn't take advantage." She'd wanted his kiss— still wanted it. Her head was buzzing with his nearness, with wanting to step into him and do it all over again.

But her bravado seemed to have left her. She lifted her chin, searching for it. "Daniel doesn't control my life."

"Doesn't he?" Seb murmured.

. . .

SEB FELT the hitch in Emma's breath just before she pressed her hand into his side. She didn't touch his knife wound or his rib, but the pressure was enough to pain both. He stepped back, breaking the connection between them.

"What is that supposed to mean?"

She'd lost the softness in her face. He would never forget the way she'd looked up at him just now, her lips pink and bee-stung from his kiss, her eyes shining.

He dragged himself across the front hall and back into the parlor. Worry for her had driven him to watch out the window, waiting for her. He'd been standing for too long and everything hurt. He moved toward the sofa.

She followed him.

"I figured it out," he said. He'd overheard the subtle way Daniel manipulated her. Like the other morning, when Emma had mentioned warming leftovers for supper, Daniel had mentioned how he'd been looking forward to Emma's shepherd's pie. When she'd offered to cook it instead of the leftovers, Daniel had hemmed and hawed and made it seem as if it was her idea to cook that night after all.

That wasn't the only example, either. Daniel had a way of getting his way with Emma. Seb had realized it must've been Daniel who'd coerced her to leave Wyoming.

"When...when you lost your sight, Daniel talked you in

to moving here." He slumped onto the sofa. When he could focus through the pain again, he saw she was shaking her head.

"That's not true."

It had to be. It was the only thing that made sense.

But Emma was still shaking her head. "Daniel didn't insist on anything. I was the one who begged him to leave Wyoming."

"No!" He slapped suddenly cold hands against his thighs.

Emma jumped. He'd startled her.

"I don't believe you." Not after the way she'd just kissed him. "You said—" It was years ago, but he'd never forget her declaration that she wanted to be with him. But he couldn't say the words aloud, not with uncertainty rolling in his gut and making him nauseated.

Her hands were trembling, and she tried to hide them under her apron, but he'd seen. "I said I loved you. And I did. But you have to understand..." Her expression beseeched him. "My entire world was turned upside down. I couldn't navigate from my bed to a chair without help. It took months for me to become comfortable in my surroundings again."

The only thing he understood right now was that she'd taken away the opportunity for him to help her through it. "I would've understood. I would've helped you. Been there for you."

Tears sparkled in her eyes. "I didn't want that." When

she spoke, her voice broke. "I didn't want to be a burden to you—to anybody. And I was afraid."

The anger he'd thought he'd buried deep inside boiled over. "You should've told me!"

She flinched at his shout.

He breathed hard. Stared at her as a tear overflowed down her cheek. She brushed it away.

"I'm sorry," she whispered.

His outburst made him feel even more ashamed. She'd made her choice, and thinking back on the kind of man he'd become, he realized she'd probably made the right one. Look at the mess he'd managed to make of his life. If she'd stayed with him, he might've ruined her life, too.

Before he could untangle his rioting thoughts, a strident knock on the door interrupted.

His body felt so heavy that the idea of standing up again seemed impossible. "Don't answer it."

She ignored his order, brushing her hand against her cheek again as she walked past the sofa. "It might be important." Drat it, her voice was still shaking. "It doesn't happen often, but occasionally one of Daniel's clients has an emergency."

He didn't want to scare her, didn't want to think that one of Tolliver's men could've tracked him here. But it wasn't outside the realm of possibility.

He forced himself up off the couch, though he was hurting so badly that he doubted he'd be able to defend her if it was one of Tolliver's thugs.

By the time he'd shuffled to the parlor door, which she'd left half open, she had the front door cracked.

"It isn't a good time, Phillip."

Phillip. The mysterious beau who'd spent hours sequestered in the kitchen with her two mornings this week. Seb hated the man, and he'd never even laid eyes on him.

Phillips said something, the words indistinguishable from where Seb stood.

And then Emma was opening the door, letting him in.

Seb's reaction time was shot, and he'd missed his chance to get back into the parlor where he wouldn't be in sight.

Phillip followed Emma into the front hall, his eyes lighting with curiosity when he caught sight of Seb.

Phillip was smartly dressed. His cheeks were smooth—almost glowing—as if he had just shaved them. His gaze was sharp, and he took in Seb quickly. No doubt he didn't miss the sickly pallor and nightclothes. Seb was the picture of an ill relative. Had Emma told her sweetheart that Seb was staying with her and Daniel?

Emma was already walking down the hall. So Seb did what he should've done before and closed the parlor door.

EMMA WAS STILL SO SHAKEN from Seb's kiss and then his temper that it was difficult to focus on Phillip.

She should've turned him away at the door, but he'd insisted it was important.

They reached the kitchen, Phillip close behind her. She stopped and turned to face him, not offering him a place to sit.

She realized he was speaking. It took some effort to focus over the cotton batting filling her head.

"I'm sorry, what did you say?" she asked.

"I asked if you were all right. There's a man in your parlor."

Seb.

Phillip was standing too close, and she realized too late that he was concerned for her.

She hadn't meant for him to find out about Seb. She must've left the parlor door open. Foolish, but she'd been so upset.

"That's my brother-in-law visiting from out of town," she said. The half-lie felt unwieldy on her tongue.

"Your brother-in-law?"

"His brother Edgar is married to Fran."

Phillip uttered a quick "huh," and she stepped back, putting more distance between them. Phillip was a friend, but she was so flustered right now that she needed the space.

"What was so important?" she asked.

"I heard back from the publisher."

"Already?" She tried to find some sadness that the publisher had so quickly found her manuscript lacking, but half her mind was still back in the parlor, arguing with Seb. "I'd like to have my manuscript back," she murmured.

"They didn't send it back. They sent a contract. And a check. They want to publish your book."

It took several seconds for the meaning of his words to sink in. Her book, in print?

"The editor also wrote that they are desperate for more quality dime novels like yours. They want to see your next manuscript as quickly as possible."

An editor wanted more of her books?

She heard Phillip's words as if from far away. She couldn't quite seem to get them to stick.

She sensed Phillip step closer, looming over her. He pressed something—a piece of paper—into her hand.

"It's your check. For five hundred dollars."

It was an impossible sum. She tried to muster some excitement to match Phillip's. The smile she gave him felt forced and unnatural. "This is so wonderful, Phillip. I can't seem to—to take it in." But not for the reasons he might suspect.

"We should celebrate." Was there a new deepness in his voice? She got that prickly feeling as if he was staring at her.

"Not tonight." She stepped away to place the check on the counter. "I'm certain Daniel will want to read the contract."

Phillip stepped into her space again, and she heard the rustle of paper settle on the counter where she'd just placed the check.

"I knew this would work out." Phillip was too close, the

heat from his body smothering her. But she'd backed herself into the counter, and there was nowhere else to go.

"That's why I sent in the manuscript," he went on, seemingly oblivious to her discomfort. "I knew you wouldn't do it, and your work deserves to be read."

His words were a reminder that it hadn't been her decision to submit the manuscript at all. She'd wanted to wait. Everything had worked out, but it hadn't been her doing. Phillip had orchestrated everything.

And somehow, that fact aggravated like a pebble in her shoe.

"Excuse me." She shifted, relieved beyond measure when he moved out of her way.

She started to lead the way back to the front door.

"Thank you for coming over to tell me the news," she said over her shoulder.

He moved more slowly, but he *did* follow. "You don't seem excited."

"I am excited." She was. She just couldn't feel anything more right now. "I'm also tired, and I need to get Daniel's supper on." And she was still reeling from the argument with Seb. She needed a moment alone. "I'll see you for our session on Tuesday," she said as she swung the front door open.

Phillip hesitated.

He was looming again, and her stomach pinched at the thought of him getting any closer.

"Thank you." She made the words sound final. "For everything."

"You're welcome," he said, his voice echoing with reluctance.

Finally, he left.

She heard Seb moving around in the parlor, but she couldn't bear to face him, not with her battered emotions confusing everything right now.

She escaped up the stairs to her room.

7

Daniel arrived home late. Seb heard him trudge up the stairs, heard a door open and the faint murmur of Emma's voice.

And then Daniel's steps came back downstairs, across the hall, and to the kitchen.

Served him right to have to scrounge for his supper. How many nights did he work late like this, leaving Emma to fend for herself? How lonely must she be, trapped here all alone?

I was the one who begged him to leave Wyoming.

Emma's words from earlier battered him, and he tossed on the sofa, aggravating his knife wound.

Hours earlier, she'd delivered his supper of bread and cheese and cold ham without a word. Her expression had been drawn, and she'd left as quickly as she'd come.

He didn't say a word to stop her.

He deserved her silence. He was an awful person. He'd

been worried about her when she'd been gone such a long time. He'd let his emotion get the better of him and kissed her, even though he'd known it was wrong.

And she'd responded so passionately.

Maybe her response had been a holdover from their shared past. Maybe she was just lonely.

Whatever had prompted her response, it wasn't genuine feelings for him. She'd made that clear when they'd argued.

Daniel entered the room, saving him from his thoughts. "You awake?"

He grunted. He had no desire to see Emma's brother right now.

But it didn't seem he had a choice as Daniel moved to sit on the chair across the room. Daniel hadn't lit a candle, and the darkness seemed oppressive around them both.

"Tolliver has been asking around about you."

Seb came instantly alert. He pushed up on his elbow.

"It's time for you to go to the sheriff."

Seb shook his head. "I can't do that."

Even in the darkness, he could sense Daniel's glare. "If you don't, he's going to keep hurting innocent people, ruining their livelihood. You know what he's capable of."

Tolliver had tried to kill Seb. Of course, he knew what the man was capable of. "If I go to the law and tell them what I did, I'll be the one sitting in jail."

Daniel's attention settled heavily on him. The question in his gaze felt obvious—why did Seb think he should be exempt from punishment when he'd done the things he had?

"Maybe so," Daniel said. "But he's hurt a lot of people."

Seb had only worked for Tolliver for a few months. Tolliver had controlled areas of Denver for years. Seb knew that Daniel was right, that the man needed to be stopped. But it wasn't Seb's job to do it, not when he'd already paid in blood by trying to get free. Not if it meant ruining his life.

He knew he wore a mulish look on his face, even if Daniel couldn't see it.

Daniel made a disgusted noise and rose from the chair. "The doctor said you would be fit to travel in two days. Nothing strenuous, but you can get on a train. I'll buy your ticket. I want you gone."

If Daniel knew what had transpired between him and Emma earlier in the day, he would've booted him out right then and there.

Seb didn't say another word as Daniel left the room. The house grew quiet, and Seb was left staring at the shadows on the ceiling.

He thought about Emma and the things she'd said. About everything he'd lost when she'd decided to walk away from him, decided he wasn't man enough to take care of her.

He didn't think he slept a wink the entire night.

.   .   .

EMMA WAS STILL STEWING over the confrontation with Seb as she rattled around in the kitchen the next morning. She didn't know of a better way to explain her decision to leave Wyoming than what she'd said the night before.

When she'd gone blind, she'd been afraid and had needed to learn to make her own way. She wasn't that frightened young woman anymore.

And she still loved him. The realization felt like salt in a half-healed wound. Because she'd walked away from Seb, and he couldn't forgive her. Now that she was ready to open her heart again, he was out of reach.

"Good morning."

She could hear the exhaustion in Daniel's voice. She wished he would take better care of himself. Wished that his late nights were not a frequent occurrence. The long hours of work took it out of him. He moved toward the table, and she brought over the plate of scrambled eggs and buttered bread she'd had warming on the stove. She returned for the coffee pot.

"The publisher Phillip contacted wants to publish my book." In between bouts of stewing over Seb, she'd also been thinking over the book publishing matter. She hadn't meant to let the news out to Daniel quite like that. But at least it was out there.

He made a noise of surprise. He cleared his throat, and she heard the slurp that meant he must have sipped his coffee. "That's wonderful."

"They sent a contract," she said. "It's there on the table if you want to look over it."

She heard the slide of paper against the wooden surface of the table. Even as a young girl, she could remember watching Daniel become engrossed as he read thousand-page legal tomes. She imagined him doing the same now, his head bent over her book contract. It gave her a few moments to steel herself.

And then she said what she meant to say. "I'm going back to Wyoming."

At first he didn't seem to hear her. There was a prolonged pause as he must've needed a moment for her words to register. "What?"

She barely resisted the urge to twist her hands in front of her. She wanted to appear confident. She straightened her shoulders. "I'm going back to Wyoming."

He sighed. "Emma, I told you that after this big case breaks—"

"After this case, you'll have another." Because that was what always happened. Daniel couldn't turn away the people who needed his help. And she didn't expect him to. But she couldn't take this anymore.

"Now that I've sold my book, I have some money and—"

"It's not about the money. Emma, you can't travel in your condition. You can't see."

"I can travel, and I'm going to."

Daniel wasn't the kind of brother who would put her under lock and key. She was determined to do this. With or without his permission.

8

Seb couldn't take his eyes off Emma as she cradled her friend's baby close. They were in Caroline's house and she was working to convince her friend to go take a nap.

She'd gone to visit Caroline in the morning and returned near lunchtime with little Bertram in her arms. She claimed the tot's mother needed a break, and when she began to gather up her things to take him back to his mom in the afternoon, Seb had found himself asking to tag along. It was only a short walk down the street. It should be safe if they didn't dawdle on the street. His wounds were healing and as long as he didn't overdo it, he could walk a bit. He needed to work on his endurance since he was leaving town soon.

Things were still strained between him and Emma, and the tensions of yesterday hadn't been resolved. But he couldn't face another afternoon of sitting alone in Daniel's parlor with only his boredom, shame, and hurt for company.

He didn't figure there was any way what was between them was going to get resolved before tomorrow morning, when he intended to hop on a train. He had no specific destination in mind, he just knew that he had to get out of town before Tolliver caught up with him.

Watching Emma bounce the baby softly, his gut twisted into a knot. Everything in him rebelled against the idea of walking away from her.

I was afraid.

He hated the thought of her being afraid. Hated that she hadn't trusted him enough to be what she needed.

I didn't want to be a burden to you.

He would've helped her. It wouldn't have been a burden.

But she hadn't wanted him enough. She hadn't even given him a chance.

Part of him felt like that four-year-old boy who'd been alone in the street. What was it about him that made people want to walk away?

But he was here now. And she was talking softly in low tones with her friend Caroline, who appeared flushed with fever. The little gal who looked to be about three was playing with wooden spoons on the floor, and her nose was running with copious amounts of snot. The boy who was maybe a year older than the girl was paging through a first-year primer, mumbling to himself. Surely he was too young to read? Maybe he was making up a story.

"I insist," said Emma, her voice strident. "You're feeling poorly, and your babies need you to get better. Go lie down."

He knew how futile it was to argue with Emma, and the poor woman didn't stand a chance. Emma shooed her into what must be a tiny bedroom at the back of the cottage.

Emma turned on him with an assessing gaze. What was she thinking?

"You're good with babies." She certainly hadn't asked a question, but he found himself almost dumbfounded as she stepped close and transferred the little one into his arms.

Emma's cheeks flushed pink, and she kept her head from tipping up toward him.

He didn't know how she sensed where the little girl sat on the floor. Maybe it was the incessant drumming of that spoon. But Emma placed a gentle hand on the girl's head as she walked past, back to the pile of dishes on the table.

"You sure you don't want to let me help with the chores?" he asked.

He knew she was capable. But it didn't seem fair for him to sit on his patootie while she did all the work.

"I'm sure that I don't want you injuring yourself after all it's taken to get you healed. Sit in the rocking chair over there and occupy the children."

He followed orders. It was a relief to settle his body into the rocking chair. He moved the baby up to his shoulder. The little one cooed and rested his head in the crook of Seb's neck. Seb held him with one hand and patted the diapered rump with the other, something he'd seen his brother Oscar do many times.

The little girl abandoned her wooden spoons and came to stand at Seb's knee.

Emma had already been outside and back, lugging a bucket of water from the pump. She poured it into a pan on the stove to heat, her back to him.

"Tell us a story!" The little girl beseeched him with puppy dog eyes. She used the back of her wrist to wipe beneath her nose.

"A story?"

The boy looked up from where he sat cross-legged on the floor. "Miss Emma always tells us stories. 'Bout cowboys and horse races and bad guys and livin' on a farm."

"And princesses," the little girl interjected.

The boy pulled a face.

Seb couldn't see Emma's expression, but he was pretty sure the pink splotches coloring her neck meant she was blushing.

He'd always known she was good with children. His brothers had a passel of kids between them, and there were always little ones around the family homestead. He'd even seen her play dolls with his sister Ida all those years ago. They'd never talked about a family of their own—they hadn't had time during their stunted courtship—but now he couldn't help but wonder. Had Emma wanted children?

Had she given up that dream? Or was it something she still wanted?

It wasn't his place to ask. She didn't want him in her life.

He cleared his throat, looking at the two expectant faces in front of him. "All right... A cowboy walked into town."

"You're supposed to say 'once upon a time' at the beginning," the boy interrupted.

Seb leveled a look on him, but the boy just returned the stare expectantly.

"Once upon a time," he started again, "a cowboy walked into town. He was on foot."

"What'd he look like?" the little girl asked. "And why didn't he have a horse?"

He glanced across the room to see Emma pouring that now-hot water into the wash bucket. She set the water pail aside, tucked next to the stove where she wouldn't trip on it.

"I don't know," he said. "I guess he had brown hair."

"What about what he was wearing? And where was the town? What was it like?"

He gritted his teeth at the additional questions. "I don't know. Clothes. A regular town." Whose story was this anyway?

"Miss Emma tells stories better'n you," the little girl said.

He couldn't help it. His gaze slipped to her again, and he saw the pink blush in her neck and face. She moved with easy grace as she took each dish from the table and scrubbed it in the sudsy water, then dried it from the towel she'd draped over her shoulder. She returned to the table with a clean dish and exchanged it for another dirty one.

"That's because she's an author," the little boy said.

His gaze was still on Emma, so he caught it when she fumbled, nearly dropping the plate she held.

She was what?

The baby moved on his shoulder, snuffling his face deeper into Seb's neck. He rubbed circles on the babe's back as he tried to process this new information.

"She writes books and everything." The little boy had his chest puffed up with pride, almost as if he were the one who'd accomplished the task.

Emma was scrubbing furiously now, maybe thinking that if she looked busy enough, he was going to let this go.

She should know better.

"That true?" he asked.

She nodded jerkily. Was she keeping her face averted on purpose?

He thought of all those hours she'd spent sequestered in the kitchen with Phillip. Was she somehow writing a book? How?

"You're really working with Philip?"

"I told you so." Her voice was slightly breathless, as if it was taking all her effort to scrub the dish she was holding. "He's a typist."

Well, wasn't that something? He never would've imagined Emma as an author. But if it was something she loved doing, why not?

Momentarily distracted from his mediocre storytelling attempt by a ladybug crawling across the floor, the two children gave him a few moments to watch Emma without any distraction.

My entire world was turned upside down.

She'd worked hard to overcome the hurdles her blindness had caused. She'd made a life for herself. She was happy here. She had Daniel to look after her, true, but she had made friends. She was writing a book, chasing her dream. And she hadn't needed Seb to make any of it happen.

He felt that yawning emptiness open up inside him again. He tried to tell himself it was a good thing that she was happy.

That he was happy for her.

But thinking about their time together two years ago choked him up, his throat tight and hot.

He wished things could've been different. Wished there could've been a place in her heart for him.

EMMA FINISHED the dishes and heated more water for Caroline's laundry. Fran had written once about how it felt like dirty clothes multiplied when she'd had a baby. Emma didn't know firsthand, but she wanted to make things easy for Caroline today, while she didn't feel well.

Seb was subdued, talking with the children in quiet tones.

She imagined him in the rocker, his broad shoulders a perfect place for the baby to snuggle in close. He would hold him securely. Seb's arms had always been a safe place.

That kind of thinking was dangerous. Seb was still angry with her, and everything was in a muddle. She'd tried to explain to him why she'd left, but she hadn't been able to make him understand.

Maybe he never would.

She'd made the best decision she could at the time. To leave Wyoming. But every decision had a consequence. Hadn't life taught her that? She thought about those dark days when she and Fran had been on the run from Underhill. She'd thought it was innocent to flirt with a man, to encourage his intentions. She's been young and stupid. Her naivety had almost cost her sister her life.

Some decisions, once made, altered the course of your life.

And it was clear that she'd hurt Seb deeply. Maybe it wasn't entirely her fault that he was now a hardened, distant person. But certainly her leaving had been a part of it.

She prayed as she washed. She prayed that he would remember how much his family loved him. She prayed that he would go back home. Or, if he couldn't go back home, that at least he would send a letter to let his family know he was all right. Tears stung behind her nose as she prayed for him to find happiness again, even if it couldn't be with her. She wasn't foolish enough to think that he could love her again, not after the way things ended between them.

She took the two older children into the tiny yard with her as she worked to pin up the dozens of cloth diapers on the line. As the afternoon wore on, the kids laughed and shrieked, chasing each other around the small space.

She was halfway through the stack of diapers when Seb joined her.

"The little guy fell asleep on me," he said. "I put him in the cradle in the bedroom."

"Caroline?"

"She didn't even stir."

She wasn't surprised. Caroline was exhausted, and Emma didn't blame her. On top of caring for three sick children, Caroline had come down with the sickness herself. Emma would do everything she could to make sure Caroline didn't have any remaining chores today.

"The kids are occupied. Why don't you let me help?" he asked.

She took half the stack of clean, damp diapers and extended them toward where his voice had come from.

He took them, his fingers clasping around her hands, lingering for a moment, holding the cloths between them.

"Emma."

Her heart thundered in her chest. But he only sighed and drew away.

"I'm going to be leaving soon," he said.

She ducked her head to reach for another cloth, hoping to hide her dismay. She'd known this was coming. But she wasn't ready.

She wanted to ask him to stay. But that wouldn't be fair. She didn't even know what was chasing him.

She heard the rustle of fabric as he clipped diapers onto the clothesline.

She swallowed and could only hope that her voice would come out even. "I believe I'm going to go on a trip as well. In a few days, after Caroline is better."

"Good for you." His voice was quiet.

She forced a smile. "It's been far too long since I've visited Fran. And your family."

The silence stretched between them, the only sound the children's chatter from across the yard.

She shouldn't... "If you're leaving anyway, maybe you should come with me. I know your family misses you something terrible."

Daniel would be furious, of course. He wasn't going to like her departure no matter what. But she was determined to make it happen.

"I can't."

"Of course you can. You simply go to the depot and purchase a ticket. And in a matter of days—"

"Too much has changed." His words rang with finality.

Did he mean that he had changed? Or that there was too much gone wrong between them?

Maybe she'd asked the question with the tiniest kernel of hope. That if they had more time together, she could make him understand. That he could find it in his heart to forgive her. Maybe he could find peace at the family homestead instead of running from whatever was chasing him now.

But his simple words obliterated that hope.

Her hand shook as she clipped the last diaper onto the line. "I think I'll start dinner. Do you mind watching those two until they're ready to come inside? Caroline will probably wake up in a bit, and then we can head home."

She started for the door before he could answer.

"Emma."

She kept going, afraid to look back. Afraid he would see the tears that were threatening.

9

They walked home in silence.

Emma had been quiet since she'd told him she was going back home.

Seb still couldn't believe she'd asked him to go with her. What would it solve to travel back to the place where his hopes had been dashed?

He was too caught up in his thoughts, not paying attention to his surroundings.

The thug was skulking in the shadow of Emma's front door, and Seb didn't see him until it was too late.

The man was taller than Seb and had forty pounds on him.

Seb had barely recovered enough to walk down the street. He was in no shape to be fighting. But his only thought was to get Emma past the ruffian and inside.

The thug was already moving towards them, and she was completely unaware.

Seb grasped her elbow, hard, and she gasped.

"Get inside and bar the door behind you."

"What?"

"Go!" Seb pushed her toward the front step and moved to head off the thug. He didn't recognize this guy. Had this hunk of flesh had been recruited after Seb's defection?

Seb watched to see if Emma made it to the door. What was taking her so long?

The big guy took a swing and Seb ducked, the punch meant for his face going wide. His side burned.

Another man moved out of the shadow at the side of the house toward the stoop, where Emma was struggling with the latch. Seb only got a half-second glance at the man, but his blood ran cold.

It was Beckett, Tolliver's right-hand man. He was known for his cruelty. Seb had once seen him break a child's arm as a threat to the kid's father. "Emma!"

Seb took a blow to the ribs, thankfully not the injured ones. He spun away from the man, his gaze back on Emma.

She hadn't made it inside. Beckett loomed over her, her arm in his meaty grip.

"Not so fast."

Seb's stomach lurched at the ice in Beckett's voice.

Emma's face was a pale smudge in the falling dark. She must be terrified. His mind strayed back to what she had gone through at fifteen. He still remembered the utter fear she'd expressed when a lunatic named Underhill had tried to kidnap her. She'd been afraid for herself and her sister Fran. This had to be bringing all of those fears back. But Emma stood still, her head up and alert. Was it worse for her that she couldn't see her attacker or a way to escape?

If they were going to get out of this, he needed to go on the offensive. He blocked his attacker's next blow, then feinted left and hit the man with an uppercut that rattled him.

He could hear Emma struggling with Beckett and then the sickening sound of flesh meeting flesh.

He felt the blow as if he were the one who'd been struck. Was she all right?

"Don't hurt her," he gritted out.

He didn't know where it came from, this surge of energy and adrenaline, focusing him like the point of a knife. He feared for Emma's safety. She was the only thing that mattered.

He danced around the next punch. Maybe he'd slowed his attacker with the blow he'd landed. He got in close, bracing for what would come, but he gave a hard, quick jab that connected with his attacker's temple. The man crumpled.

Seb whirled to the doorstep. Beckett had Emma trapped against the wall. His fist was coiled to strike.

There was no way Seb was going to get over there in time. He tried anyway, knowing he would be too late to block the punch.

But Emma moved, and Beckett's fist hit the closed door. The man let out a grunt of pain. He bent over slightly, and

Emma head-butted him, connecting with his nose. There was a sickening crunch.

But even that wasn't enough to make Beckett release his hold on her arm. He'd been slowed for all of two seconds, but that fist was still moving. Seb stepped in front of it and took it on the jaw, momentarily disoriented. He pushed Emma away, breaking Beckett's hold on her.

He saw her stumble and then heard her fall in the grass. Anger and desperate fear drove him until he could think of nothing else.

He slammed the heel of his hand into Beckett's face, in the same spot where Emma's headbutt had already caused blood to flow.

Beckett cried out.

But the man was tough, and he threw a fist into Seb's side, hitting the knife wound.

Seb bit back a cry. But he didn't stop fighting. He struck again and again.

"You tell... Tolliver... to stay away from her."

Seb knew the words were a mistake when Beckett's eyes gleamed with an unholy light.

He'd just given Tolliver—through Beckett—ammunition. The knowledge that Emma was important to him.

And these were exactly the kind of men who would hurt Emma to get to Seb.

He couldn't let that happen. Fury drove him, and red took over his vision. He connected punch after punch until Beckett was lying on the ground, unconscious. Even then, he couldn't make himself stop striking the man's battered face.

Not until he heard Emma's tiny voice calling his name.

EMMA LAY ON THE GROUND, terrified.

She was frozen in the grass, trembling like a baby bunny trying to hide in plain sight. Even her voice was frozen inside her, the terror of so long ago mingling with the present.

What should she do? Should she try to run?

She heard the sickening sounds of two men grunting in pain as their blows connected. A rapid flurry of movement, and then it was only the sound of one.

Smack.

Smack.

Smack.

Somehow, a punch sounded more brutal than a slap. A fist against flesh. The blows began to slow, but Emma's heart raced.

Had Seb fallen? Was she alone out here? She hadn't even been able to get inside the house like he had told her to do.

Thinking about how weak and frail he'd been over the last few days, fear for him pushed through her fright. She'd heard at least two men. With him being so injured, how could he fend off two attackers?

She murmured his name. The sickening sounds

stopped. There was only the sound of one person's harsh breathing. Was it Seb, or her assailant?

She sensed the man unfold to his full height, and footsteps brought him closer to her. All she could do was cower in the grass.

"How badly are you hurt?"

Seb.

It turned out she did have some strength left. She untangled her skirts from around her feet and stood, throwing herself at him. He caught her tightly to him, and she felt the tremors shaking him. Shaking them both.

"Come here."

He pulled her around the side of the house, where they couldn't be seen from the street. He touched her jaw, turning her face up toward his. She couldn't help wincing as his fingers brushed the place at the edge of her cheek where she'd been hit. His hand gentled.

She heard air move between his teeth in a little hiss. "He hit you?"

She didn't answer. He could probably already see the bruise blooming there.

"What else? Did you twist your ankle when I knocked you down?"

She shook her head. Other than the headache she had from head-butting her attacker, she was only shaken.

Seb pulled her closer, pressing his cheek against the top of her head. She turned her face into his throat.

"You remembered how to fight back."

She would never forget the lessons he had given her

back when Underhill had been chasing her and Fran. She hadn't known they were burned into her body's memories until she had just done it. She'd been shocked when her knee to the man's groin had hurt him.

It had been enough to give her the courage to try the headbutt as well.

Seb was holding her so tightly that she didn't have good leverage, but she patted her hands against his midsection, trying to feel for warm, sticky blood.

"Did they reopen your wounds? Are you hurt?"

She felt his chin brush her hair as he shook his head. "If I am, I don't feel it."

She wasn't sure how that was possible. Maybe he just didn't want to tell her.

He let her go, and she felt the loss of his touch keenly.

"We've got to go."

Go? Go where?

"Those two are out for now, but they'll rouse soon enough."

She felt a weird sense of relief. He hadn't killed that awful man. The sounds of his punches, fist hitting flesh, were burned into her memory, and she shuddered.

He didn't embrace her this time.

"Where are we going?"

He took her arm and ushered her down the street. "It's not safe here. They knew where to find me. They know where you live. We've got to get to Daniel."

Air froze in her lungs. "Do you think Daniel is in danger?"

His step stuttered, but he pressed on. "I hope not. Daniel can keep you safe."

"What—what about you? You protected me."

He laughed, the sound bitter. "I'm the reason those thugs attacked us. You wouldn't have been in danger tonight if it weren't for me."

"So you're leaving?" Her voice emerged tiny. She hated what it revealed to him. That she still had feelings for him.

He was silent for a moment, their footsteps the only sound between them. Finally, he said, "I was always planning to leave, remember? But I can promise you won't be in danger again."

She heard the tone of resolve in his voice. What did that mean?

"What are you going to do?"

"Something Daniel's been after me to do. Something I was trying to get out of doing. I'm not running away anymore."

"Daniel and I will help you."

"This is something I've got to do myself."

"But—"

"Emma, this is hard enough. Don't you understand?"

Suddenly he stopped walking and tugged her around so they were face-to-face. He crushed her to him again, his mouth pressing against hers in a desperate kiss. In his kiss, she felt everything. The love still between them—it hadn't died after all. His desperation and fear. He was pouring everything he felt into this one last kiss. As if he was saying good-bye forever.

Some noise must've spooked him, because he broke the kiss and held her close for another second before he let her go, taking her arm again and moving down the street.

After what she'd been through, she understood why he felt he needed to go on alone.

But she hadn't been alone. Not really. She'd had Daniel by her side.

Who would stand by Seb?

PART II

10

1906 - A small Wyoming town

C ecilia White's heart pounded as she waited for the last of her students to trickle out of the classroom.

All except Joel.

Joel was one of the younger students, and his father picked him up every day after school.

Cecilia couldn't help the way her hands trembled as she piled up the school books she was going to take home with her tonight. Her lunch pail was empty and sat on top of her desk. She wiped down the blackboard and then quickly swept up the dried grass and dust her students had brought in with them after the recess break.

There were two more weeks before the summer break.

Two more weeks of seeing her students grasp a new

concept for the first time. Seeing the pride on their faces and knowing that she was the one teaching them.

It was a source of pride that she could begin to pay back the long-overdue debt that she owed her parents.

She loved being a teacher, but today she could barely focus on the usual end-of-day tasks.

Because Joel's father Simon was coming to pick him up.

And if it happened the same way it had happened for the past three weeks, Simon would ask if they could walk home together.

It was completely innocent. She was a teacher who had to walk home, and Simon and Joel happened to be walking in the same direction.

But the stolen moments with Simon as Joel ran ahead were quickly becoming some of Cecilia's most cherished times. Simon was charming and handsome and a good father...

And here.

But when Cecilia turned to see the schoolhouse door open, it was not Simon who entered.

She stiffened at the sight of Mr. Potter, one of the school board members who had hired her at the beginning of the school term.

He spotted Joel waiting quietly at the corner desk.

"Run along now, child," Mr. Potter said. "Your papa's waiting for you outside."

Cecilia's stomach swooped and twisted. What was going on?

"I'm surprised to see you today, sir." She moved to the desk and picked up her books and pail.

Mr. Potter's expression was serious, his frown stretched across his entire face. "We need to talk, young lady."

She put her books and pail down. His tone heightened her anxiety. Should she sit? Was he here to extend her an invitation to teach next year? She'd gotten rave reviews about the school's Christmas pageant, and the spelling bee had been well-attended only a few weeks before. One of her students was even planning to attend college in the fall.

Dithering, she finally settled her hip against the desk.

He stood with arms crossed in the middle of the classroom.

"The school board informed you that there would be no tolerance for improper behavior."

Cecilia's neck went hot even as her hands went cold. That did not sound like a promising start. What could he be referencing? She'd been very careful to keep her actions appropriate at all times.

Mr. Potter seemed as if he were waiting for her to speak, but she had no idea what to say. "I remember," she said when it seemed he would not go on without her acknowledging his words.

"If you remember our conversation, then I have to say that I am surprised by the way you have been comporting yourself."

She shook her head. "May I ask what specifically you are speaking of?"

"Have you been spending time with the father of one of your students?"

The heat in her face and neck intensified. "If you mean Simon, we have walked together on our way home a few times. Surely it's not inappropriate to walk home with one of my students and his parent."

Joel's father was a widower. What could be inappropriate in having a simple conversation as they walked in the same direction?

Mr. Potter wore an expression of keen disappointment. "Simon is married. It is shameful for you to attempt to break up a family."

Cecilia's confusion grew. "He told me his wife had passed away."

Mr. Potter only frowned more as if her words were some kind of admission of guilt. "His first wife passed away. He remarried, and I believe his second wife is in the family way." He spoke the last in nearly a whisper, as if the admission itself was inappropriate. "She's been bedridden these last months."

Unease boiled in Cecilia's stomach. Simon had told her his wife died, but not that he had remarried. What could he have possibly meant by withholding the information?

"Be that as it may," she said. "Is there a rule against walking with a child and his parent home from school?"

"Of course not. But Joel's mother saw you out the window talking with her husband and thought you looked too familiar. She said you were flirting with him."

Cecilia may have smiled at Simon, but she hadn't so

much as touched him. She'd never been alone in his presence. Joel had always accompanied them.

She told Mr. Potter all of this.

But he shook his head, and his frown remained. "The school board put me in charge of this matter to take a statement from all of the parties involved. Simon indicated that you had been the one to suggest walking home together. He also indicated that you had made overtures toward him."

Cecilia's throat closed up, but she forced words past her suddenly dry tongue. "That is not true. And if he thought I was, why did he continue to walk with me?"

Mr. Potter didn't have an answer. And she couldn't tell whether he believed her.

He made her sit down, and they went through every interaction that she could remember having had with Simon, no matter how innocent. Every time they had walked home together. What Simon had said to her.

As she recounted their friendship, each thing that she had to tell Mr. Potter made shame color her cheeks.

Her actions hadn't been inappropriate. Perhaps she had flirted with Simon at times, but he had led her to believe that he was single. Surely Mr. Potter and the other board members couldn't find fault with her behavior.

But as Mr. Potter ended his line of questioning, she saw disappointment, and even anger etched in his expression.

"I did nothing wrong." She tried to sound confident, but she heard desperation in her tone.

"I am very disappointed. The school board cautioned you against acting inappropriately."

She swallowed hard, felt a stinging behind her nose that meant tears were close. She fought them back.

"We were never alone. Joel was always with us. Every single moment."

Mr. Potter shook his head "When one of the mothers from our community makes an accusation like the one Simon's wife made, what do you think the other mothers are going to believe of a teacher they've only known for a few months?"

Her reputation would be shattered. Mama would be ashamed of her. She was ashamed of herself. The pride and hope she'd felt an hour ago were completely gone.

"Are you firing me?"

"It is too late to find a replacement. You will stay on through the end of the school year, but you'll leave immediately after the last day."

How humiliating. To be treated like a child. Even if he believed her, he was treating her as if she had done something wrong.

"And a recommendation?" she whispered. "So I can find a new job for next term?"

He only shook his head.

11

Six Weeks Later - Bear Creek, Wyoming

Seb was going home.

It had been just over a year since he had last seen Emma. A little over twelve months since she had shared her disappointment over his not communicating with his parents.

He'd sent one letter home ahead of him. They'd have received it over a month ago now. He'd wanted to let his parents know he was coming. If they disowned him or turned him away, it would be no less than he deserved. But just in case his parents had a shred of love left for him, he'd sent the letter to prepare them.

It had taken him this long to get free of the mess with Tolliver. He didn't regret any of it. Well, maybe getting tangled up with Tolliver in the first place.

He planned to spend some time at home and try not to

ask Fran in the first ten seconds whether Emma had found someone new and gotten married. He'd left her without a good-bye. It hadn't been ideal, but once he'd delivered her to Daniel and said a few words to the man, Daniel had put him in touch with a US marshal, who had whisked him away into a safe house that same night.

Even if he'd had a chance to say good-bye, he wouldn't have asked Emma to wait for him. It wouldn't have been fair. Emma deserved someone who hadn't made the mistakes Seb had.

But if by some chance she was still unmarried, well... He aimed to show her how trustworthy he could be now.

He reined in his horse at the top of a small plateau. It wasn't far now. Another two miles. Not long until he would look his parents in the face and find out whether they could forgive him for running away.

He still wasn't sure whether he was going to bring up Tolliver and everything else that had transpired. Not immediately, that was for sure.

He felt peaceful, just being back in Wyoming. The Laramie Mountains in the distance were a sight that he'd grown up with. One that was the backdrop for so many fond memories of his childhood.

The morning air was crisp but promised warmth for later in the day.

He studied the landscape around him, looking for changes. Most everything looked about the same as he remembered. He was the one who'd changed. And only a few of those changes were on the outside.

A small homestead rested in a pretty little valley to the west. A house, corral, and barn. There was someone out there—a woman—hanging clothes on the line. She raised her hand to shield her eyes as she looked his way.

He tried to remember who lived out this way. Seemed like it was Cora Beth, a girl he'd known as a youngster. She'd married another boy from their class. Seb waved his hand. Today wasn't the day to stop and chat about their school days.

But something strange happened when she caught sight of him. Her arm dropped to her side. She turned and left her wash behind and darted across the yard and into her house. All within the span of a few seconds.

It wasn't his business. He should keep on heading toward home.

But something about the moment bothered him.

He took visual stock of her homesteaded. The roof over the front porch was sagging, one of the corner posts missing. Her tiny lean-to barn needed a paint job. The horse in the corral was in fine shape, but the field that should be coming up with summer wheat was empty, unplowed.

He felt a sudden tug in his gut. A need to check on her. Why would she run like that?

He rode down to the house but reined in several yards away when she shouted from the cracked window.

"I told you that if you came back I was gonna shoot you!"

Her shout surprised him. He held up his hands, dropping the reins. He'd been on the road for several days, but he didn't think his whiskers and trail dust were *that* bad. "Cora Beth, it's Seb White. Are you all right?"

"Seb? Seb White ain't been home in three years."

Her voice was unsure. Maybe he was imagining it, but he thought she wanted to believe him.

He moved one hand and knocked his hat back so she could get a better look at his face. "It's me. I'm heading home right now. I saw you take off for your house and figured maybe I should check on you."

He heard a sound like a sob, and that was enough for him to lower his hands and get out of the saddle.

He put his hands up in front of himself again just in case she got any ideas. "I'm coming up to the door. I just want to check on you."

Another sob from inside.

He made it to the door without her firing at him. He knocked. She opened it, then stood back, her arms wrapped around her middle. Her face was tear-stained.

"I'll stay out here if it makes you feel better."

"You can have a cup of coffee." She said the words with a little hiccup.

"That would be nice." He'd been eager to get home, but now he sat at a little table between the kitchen and the neatly-made bed in the corner. He put his hands on the table to show her he wasn't going to try anything.

The furnishings were sparse and worn. Her quilt was threadbare. Almost as threadbare as her dress, which had been patched so much he couldn't figure what the original fabric had looked like.

She set the cup of coffee in front of him with shaking hands. She didn't have a cup for herself. But she did sit across from him. Almost folded into herself, crossed her arms over her chest, and seemed much smaller than she really was.

He raised one eyebrow and glanced toward the window that was still cracked. "I don't see a rifle."

She shrugged. "It's under the bed. I don't got no bullets for it anyway."

He took a sip of coffee. "Who's been bothering you?"

Her lips pinched.

He took a different tack. "Where's your man?" Maybe that would explain why the place was in such disrepair and why she was so scared. Had she been abandoned out here?

"He was—he passed about eighteen months ago. He was trying to fell a tree that was too big for him to handle." She swallowed hard, tears building in her eyes again.

"Hasn't anyone come around to help you?" It wasn't like the town of Bear Creek to let one of their own suffer. The community usually rallied around anyone in need. Barn raisings, collecting money, even sewing bees for families who couldn't afford new clothing. How come Cora Beth was in such dire straits?

"There was a bad drought last year," she said. "Folks around here are having a hard time." Her chin jutted upward stubbornly. "I'm not gonna take charity from folks who can scarcely afford to give it."

He hadn't realized about the drought. Like she said,

he's been gone too long. Had his parents lost their crop? They ran a lot of cattle. If their crops hadn't come in, Pa might be having trouble feeding all the animals this year.

"I'm sure your family is waiting to see you. I appreciate you stopping by."

Seemed like she intended to dismiss him, but he could still hear her soft sob in his head. "I'll go just as soon as you tell me what's got you so scared."

She sighed. Her eyes cut up to him and then back down to stare at the table. They'd known each other for a long time. She knew how stubborn he could be. He waited her out. It didn't take long.

"I don't know his name. He only came around once. He was on foot. I was tending the garden and didn't hear him approach until he was standing right over me." She shivered. "It was the way he looked at me. There was pure evil in his eyes. It scared me bad. I told him my man was hunting for our supper and would be back soon. He left, but not before telling me he hoped my man was a good shot. He might've been talking about hunting, but I took his meaning another way."

Seb had had enough experience with men like she was talking about. He didn't need to know this one personally to believe what she was saying. Cora Beth had always had a good head on her shoulders. If she was scared, then she had a reason to be.

"Did he come back?"

She scratched one fingernail against the tabletop. "I started keeping a better watch. Two of my chickens disappeared without a trace. No feathers, not like something had gotten into the henhouse. No squawking in the middle of the night. A week ago, I thought I saw a man skulking around in that copse of trees on the hill. He never came out of the shadows, but..."

But she felt like he'd been watching her.

"I shouted out about shooting him if he came back," she finished.

"You can't stay here."

Her eyes flashed up at him. "I ain't got nowhere to go."

"You've got no ammunition. I'm willing to bet your larder is empty. And someone's been stalking you."

"This is my home. What am I supposed to do?"

He didn't know. Didn't know how to fix this for her. But he knew who would.

"Why don't you come home with me?

When she started to shake her head, he pressed on. "Just for a visit. My ma always enjoys chatting with a friend. And I'm sure Pa won't mind if you *borrow*"—he put extra emphasis on the word—"some ammunition. They may even loan you a few groceries. Until you can get back on your feet."

He knew how prideful people could be. She didn't want charity.

But he wasn't leaving her out here alone and scared.

"Help you, young lady?" Earl asked.

"No, I'm just browsing." Emma let her fingers play

along the bolts of fabric. The mercantile was bustling with customers today, and the press of people made it difficult for her to navigate.

"You sure?" The mercantile owner sounded skeptical.

Emma nodded. She'd only been in tiny Bear Creek for two months. The people here were still getting used to working around her limitations. But they were friendly and—mostly—helpful.

Fran and Edgar had stopped asking whether they should help Emma with the smallest tasks on the very first day she'd arrived. Home.

Home.

She was really and truly home. She felt like she belonged. Not like in Denver, where she'd started to feel like a guest in Daniel's house. It had taken her longer to leave than she'd planned.

Caroline had hit a hard patch, and Emma had stayed to help her. She'd stayed so long and had eventually involved Daniel. Since then, her brother had fallen helplessly in love with Caroline. They'd been married the week before Emma left.

Upon Emma's arrival back home, she'd fallen in love with her niece Eloise and new nephew Henry.

The only thing missing was Seb.

Seb, whom she prayed for daily.

Seb, who hadn't written to her or tried to contact her.

He'd simply disappeared.

But she didn't stop hoping he would return home.

She wasn't alone in her hope. His entire family wanted him back, no one more than his mother, Penny.

Speaking of his family, where were Susie and Velma? The sisters had been adopted by Oscar and Sarah, Seb's oldest brother, years ago. Velma was a precocious twelve-year-old, while Susie was nineteen and...

Emma listened for them now and picked up voices.

Susie was flirting with the shopkeeper's son. If she focused, Emma could hear the trill of her laugh through the murmur of other customers' voices, the jingle of something metal, and an exclamation from one of the older men sitting near the potbelly stove, where they played checkers and gossiped like old hens.

Relief settled. She didn't know where Velma was, but Susie hadn't abandoned her.

Emma had never been close with Susie. Susie was a bright, vivacious force of nature. Like a cyclone, she sucked up all the energy of a room. Sometimes stormed like booming thunder.

While Emma didn't mind fading into the background.

Which suited her just fine, at least until the store cleared out a bit.

She made her way past the bolts of fabric and the dry goods and loitered near the window display.

She couldn't help reaching out... yes. It was still there. Fran had commented on the fine lace shawl several Sunday mornings ago. The mercantile wasn't open on Sundays, but the window display had drawn Fran's attention as the family wagon had carried them out of town.

Emma had been drawn to the shawl on her next trip to town.

The lace was almost as soft as a kitten's fur.

A floorboard squeaked, and one footstep was all the warning Emma had before Velma's arm brushed her elbow.

"Are you gonna buy that?"

Emma dropped her hand from the shawl. "It's not very practical, is it?" The lace would catch easily on a cabinet knob or a wicker basket. It was far too fancy for life on a ranch.

"And it's expensive," Velma whispered.

That too. Emma could purchase it. But if she did, everyone would want to know where she'd gotten the money.

And she wasn't ready for everyone to know her secret yet.

"Not today," she said to the girl. She was ready to go home after several hours dictating with Phillip. Her friend had traveled to Wyoming for the week so that Emma could write the next book that her publisher demanded. Susie and Velma had accompanied her to town. Now Emma was worn out and ready to go home.

She said as much to Velma, and the younger sister managed to pry her flirtatious older sister from the shop-keeper's soon.

On the boardwalk, Susie paused. Then gasped.

"What is it?" Emma's heart clanged against her ribs. She was more on edge since the night she and Seb had been attacked. Daniel had told her that the criminal who'd sent thugs after Seb wasn't going to be an issue anymore, but she couldn't help being startled.

"I think it's... Seb!"

Susie's sudden cry made Emma's ear ring. And then Susie's word registered.

"It's him," Velma said from Emma's side. "He's coming this way."

"But who's that with him?" Susie said under her breath.

"What?" Emma's pulse raced. She was having trouble following the conversation.

"He's with a woman. Someone I don't recognize," Susie murmured.

And then there was no more time for questions, because Emma heard boots striking the boardwalk.

"Seb!" Velma's excitement was evident in her voice. Emma felt motion as if the younger girl had thrown herself at her uncle.

He laughed, the sound as comforting and familiar as the fire in the hearth.

Emma realized she hadn't heard the sound once in those few days they'd been together in Denver. She'd missed it.

"Look at you. You've grown about a foot since I saw you last. Hello, Susie."

Susie moved, and Emma guessed she was hugging him.

She knew she was blushing by the burning heat in her face. "Hello, Seb."

"Emma." His voice revealed nothing. Was he happy to see her? Did she make him uneasy?

She'd told him in Denver that she was coming back to the homestead. Was he surprised?

She wished he would give her some clue. And who was with him?

A skirt swished in the awkward silence that fell.

Emma felt heat in her earlobes.

"Y'all remember Cora Beth? She and I went to school together."

"But what's she doing with y—?"

Velma's impertinent question cut off in a yelp. Knowing the sisters as she did, she guessed Susie'd pinched her little sister. Emma wouldn't put it past her.

Emma couldn't be sure, but the awareness at the back of her neck usually meant someone was staring at her. Was it Seb? Or his...? Or Cora Beth?

Emma almost wished Velma had finished her question. Then she'd know who Cora Beth was to him. Was she a friend? Or something more?

She hadn't been prepared for this. Every time she'd imagined Seb returning to the homestead, he'd been alone. Sometimes happy to see her. Sometimes still hard and distant, as he'd been in Denver.

But always alone.

She didn't know what to think. She couldn't seem to gather her thoughts into any semblance of order.

"Y'all heading home?" Seb asked.

"Yes," Susie said. Then slyly added, "As long as Emma's done sparkin' with her beau."

"Susie!"

The ornery young woman knew well enough that when Emma spent time with Phillip, it was work. But she persisted in teasing that there was something more going on.

"As a matter of fact, we are returning to the homestead," Emma said to Seb.

Jonas had built the original cabin on the homestead years ago when the boys had been young. When each brother had come of age, they'd filed for their own property on adjoining land and as they'd married, some of them had built their own homes nearby. Now the homestead was a compound. Oscar, Edgar, Matty, and Davy, along with their respective families, each had a home on the family property.

"Mind if we ride alongside? Our horses are tied off by the hotel."

"Your ma and pa are going to be so happy to see you!" Velma bounced on her toes, the motion moving the boardwalk boards beneath Emma's feet.

"Huh." Seb made a sound that could've been agreement or disagreement. She wished she could see his face. She wanted to know what he was feeling, coming home after all this time. Of course, maybe it wasn't her business.

"Oh, I bet Grandma Penny is going to cook a big meal tonight to celebrate," Velma said. "I know! Wait for me, just for a minute. I'm gonna run over to the clinic and tell Maxwell 'n Hattie."

The girl was off before anyone could get a word in edgewise.

Seb's voice came from further away. "Does she remind anybody else of Breanna?"

"Every single day." Emma felt the jostle of his elbow against hers and didn't know if it was intentional, if he was trying to share the moment of levity with her. Or whether it was a complete accident, simply a product of standing near.

He cleared his throat. "I'll go get the horses and meet you at the wagon. Cora Beth, you all right?"

The woman must have made some sign—a nod, or a smile—because Seb hopped off of the boardwalk, his footsteps in the dirt lane quickly fading.

Which left Emma with the ornery Susie, and Seb's... Cora Beth.

"Do you think Jonas and Penny will mind me interrupting Seb's homecoming?" Cora Beth asked softly.

Susie inhaled deeply, and Emma was worried about what she would say. Seb wouldn't want his niece to embarrass Cora Beth.

"They'll be delighted," Emma said quickly, and firmly.

And if she wasn't delighted, only confused and fighting with her tangled emotions during the wagon ride home, well, that was another matter.

12

E mma thought she had come to accept losing her sight. She'd grieved the loss. She'd experienced anger and even denial in the very beginning.

She was content. Or at least she had been, until tonight.

When they'd arrived back at the homestead in the afternoon, Penny must have seen them from the window because she'd run out of the house, calling Seb's name and crying for joy. Cora Beth had stood nearby. Emma and Susie and Velma had excused themselves as his mother wept over his return. He'd kept quiet about Cora Beth's presence. He had to have. The family was a nosy bunch and if he'd announced any kind of intentions about Cora Beth, everyone would've been talking about it.

True to Velma's prediction, Penny had immediately gotten to work in the kitchen. She'd recruited her daughters-in-law to help as much as they could, and now the family was spread out at three large picnic tables outside the original family home.

Emma had a shawl wrapped around her shoulders. The sun was setting and the night just beginning to have the slightest chill.

Everyone wanted to crowd close around Seb. Since Emma had walked over with Edgar and Fran and their little ones, Walt and Andrew had been stuck to him like glue. Ida had climbed into his lap until her mom had moved her across the table from where Seb and Cora Beth sat. Penny and Jonas were on his left. His older brother Oscar and Sarah and their youngest were also at the first table.

Which meant Emma was relegated to the middle table with Edgar and Fran and their two little ones. Baby Henry, named after Emma and Fran's father, was sleeping, snug against Emma's shoulder. She'd taken the easier job, because three-year-old Eloise could make a mess at the dinner table in under a minute flat if you weren't paying close enough attention. Emma was happy to let Fran wrangle her as Edgar tried to lean over from his seat and get in on the ribbing Seb's brothers were giving him.

The jumble of voices and silverware tinking against plates, the shrieks from the children when one of them stole someone else's last scoop of mashed potatoes. All of it combined and made it almost impossible for Emma to focus on Seb's voice. She still didn't know if Cora Beth was someone special to him. She must be. He'd brought her home with him, hadn't he? Much as she wanted to ask,

Emma wouldn't break in on Seb's precious time with his family. Not when it would make her the center of attention. Not when she was so uncertain about where she stood in his life.

"Are you sure you're feeling all right?" Fran asked. "No, don't scoop up the potatoes with your hand—" It took Emma a moment to realize she must be speaking to Eloise. And then to Emma once again. "You've been quiet all afternoon."

"I'm fine. I must've used up all my words telling my new story to Phillip today."

Emma hoped Fran would believe her. Fran didn't know about Emma's long-ago relationship with Seb. No one had until she'd been forced to tell Daniel when he'd demanded to know why it was such a rush for them to leave Wyoming.

And if Cora Beth was someone special to Seb, Daniel would remain the only one to know.

She'd hoped Seb would come home eventually. She just hadn't expected it to be with someone else by his side.

"I'm not sure I'm comfortable with you spending so much time with Phillip alone."

"What? Why?" Emma couldn't keep a half-laugh from her voice at Fran's words. "We're not alone. We sit in the hotel dining room, in full view of anyone who walks by."

"I don't know how you talked Daniel into it. I've seen the way that Phillip looks at you. I can't believe that Daniel encouraged—unless he's truly so oblivious that he didn't know…"

Emma let her sister's prattle roll over her. Until his visit this week, it'd been months since she'd spent time with Phillip. This was the fourth book that Emma had sold to the publisher. And it was almost done. She only needed one more day.

Her publisher had wanted to use an alias, claiming that they would sell more books if her identity remained a secret. Emma didn't care one way or the other, and she'd capitulated. Daniel, and now Fran and Edgar, were the only ones who knew that she'd authored three, soon to be four, dime novels. She sort of felt like Fran and Edgar humored her. She hadn't told them exactly how much money she had saved up in her bank account. She'd only told Susie that she was working with Phillip and after Susie's display earlier today, she knew she'd have to give the girl something more or be subjected to more teasing comments.

When her next check arrived, she'd planned to ask whether she could buy a bit of land from Jonas and build her own house close by Fran and Edgar. But Seb's sudden reappearance had flipped her world upside down.

The baby stirred, snuffling into Emma's shoulder. She rubbed his back, a slow soothing circle that usually put him back to sleep. But not now. He was waking up, and Emma knew he would be hungry.

Eloise shrieked, and Fran groaned under her breath. "I think it's time we took these two home and put them to bed."

Edgar started to say something, but Fran shushed him. "Emma and I can take care of the little ones tonight."

She knew Fran didn't mean anything by speaking for her. Fran didn't know how much Seb meant to Emma. What she'd suggested made sense.

Edgar was Seb's brother. He had the most right to be here.

Seb might have made declarations to her all those years ago, but she was the one who'd broken the promises. When he'd reappeared in her life in Colorado, there'd been no promises spoken between them.

She had no claim on Seb. And no reason to protest as Fran stood up and started making noises about leaving, saying good night to everyone.

The baby was starting to cry softly now. Emma knew how quickly his cries could turn into earsplitting wails. She had used her walking stick to navigate the walk from Fran and Edgar's cabin to the main house. Now, she scooped it up from under her chair and stood, using it to make sure she didn't trip on any of the chairs as she made her way from the picnic tables and followed Fran.

She kept silent on the walk, berating herself for the disappointment filling her heart. What has she expected? For Seb to get up and chase her away from the table? His brothers were nosy jokesters, and they could tease a body until you wanted to scream. If Seb had asked to speak with her later or in private, everyone would've seen. Besides, he had Cora Beth now.

Fran wouldn't be able to see Emma's face in the dark.

And so if she shed a tear or two, she only tilted her face and used the baby's blanket to wipe them away. By the time she and Fran arrived home, she had herself under control.

SEB STOOD in the open doorway of his parents' kitchen, staring out into the darkness. Was Emma settled in at Fran and Edgar's place? Was she thinking of him tonight, wondering, like he was?

Did she have a beau? Susie had been teasing when she'd mentioned it in town—he was almost sure of it.

But what if it hadn't been a joke.

He wanted so badly to go to her and find out for himself.

But between his ma's happy tears and the emotion Pa hadn't been afraid to show, the timing was wrong. And during supper, he'd gotten drawn into all manner of conversations with his brothers. He hadn't missed the moment when she and Fran had left to take care of the two babies. He'd even thought about going after her, but he couldn't leave Cora Beth alone with his rowdy family.

Cora Beth now stood at the washtub with his mother. She'd insisted on helping clean up after the meal.

Jonas and Maxwell were speaking in low tones just outside. Seb couldn't hear the words they spoke. The moon had come up, and Maxwell and Hattie were planning to drive their wagon back to town tonight. Both were doctors, and they had a busy day of taking care of patients ahead of them tomorrow.

Oscar appeared out of the darkness, moving past Seb in the doorway and slapping him on one shoulder.

"What're they talking about?" Seb asked, jerking his chin to indicate his pa and brother.

Oscar frowned. "Someone started a rumor in town about him and Hattie overcharging for their services."

Seb scoffed.

"Exactly," Oscar said. "Half the time they take a trade instead of the cash that they need. Hattie had a pantry full of onions all summer because it was the only way Mrs. Oliver could afford to pay her."

They both knew that Maxwell and Hattie would work for free if they could afford it. And that they would forgive the debt owed by any of the people they doctored. But folks in Bear Creek were stubborn. They didn't want to be beholden to anybody or to take charity. So a trade was a way to make things fair for both parties.

Jonas appeared out of the darkness, and he, too, put a hand to Seb's shoulder. Seb had been receiving hugs and handshakes and shoulder grips from his family all night. It was something he hadn't let himself miss. Something he hadn't let himself think about, that easy affection they shared. But now that he was on the receiving end of it, he realized just how empty his life has been these past few years.

They sat inside at the long kitchen table where Seb could remember doing sums on a slate as a schoolboy.

Penny glanced over her shoulder from the washtub. "We're almost finished here. Do you want us to take a cup of coffee in the sitting room?"

Seb shook his head. He'd told his parents earlier that he needed to talk about Cora Beth. It was good that his oldest brother had stuck around as well. "I'd like you to be here too, Ma."

The two women finished up with the dishes and joined the men at the table, wiping their hands on aprons.

"I rode by Cora Beth's place on my way home today."

He shared a look with the woman, who'd had a tiny bit of light return to her eyes tonight under the care of his Ma and siblings. He wasn't going to tell his family just how frightened she been.

"She's had a rough time of it lately. And I know a lot of folks around here have too." He hadn't had a chance yet to talk to his father about how things were around the ranch. Whatever needed doing, he intended to do it.

"It's not just the drought and tough times, though. She's had a man sniffing around her place, threatening her."

Oscar and Jonas bristled. Penny laid her hand over Cora Beth's on the table.

"Who is it?" Oscar asked. "I'm sure between Matty and us, we can set things right."

Cora Beth was biting her lip, some of the tension back in her shoulders now. "He didn't tell me a name. I didn't recognize him. I've been too afraid to ride to town alone, thinking he might catch me unawares out in the open. If Seb hadn't come along..."

It didn't bear thinking about.

"But you're safe now, dear," Penny said. Seb had always appreciated his mother's gentle touch and her protective nature. Tonight he appreciated it a little bit more.

Cora Beth blushed and looked at the table. "Being with you all tonight has made me remember everything I've been missing since Roy died. I was thinking maybe I should go stay with my aunt Martha in California for a while." She looked up, her eyes landing on Seb and then bouncing to Jonas and then Penny. "I don't have money for a train ticket, but I do have the horse. He's a good working animal. And I've got a few chickens still left at home."

Jonah shook his head. "If you decide you want to sell your animals, that'll be up to you. But we're more than happy to pay for your train ticket. And I won't hear another word about it."

Cora Beth's eyes filled with tears, and she had to cover her face with her apron for a moment. After she pulled herself together, she smiled a tremulous smile. "I'll never stop thanking God for sending Seb my way today."

"Seb and I can ride over to your place with you tomorrow," Oscar said. "You can pack a bag, gather anything you need, and we can bring your chickens over here to take care of them while you're gone. If you decide you want to sell them later, you can send word."

Penny put her arm around the younger woman. "Let's go make up the extra bed in Ida's room."

Seb felt a stirring of pride in his family. He'd known that whether or not they were happy to see him, they wouldn't let Cora Beth down.

He still couldn't believe the reception he had gotten. The prodigal returning after all these years. Of course, his parents didn't know about the trouble he's gotten himself into in Denver. The things he'd done and the price he'd paid to get out of trouble. Maybe it would change the way Jonas looked at him if he ever found out. Seb had been vague about where he'd been. He hadn't made one mention of making a living with his fists. Maybe being home was enough. Maybe he didn't have to tell them everything.

The sound of Penny's voice faded as she led Cora Beth to the back of the house.

Oscar gave Jonas a meaningful look, but Seb couldn't read whatever message went between the two men.

Jonas's face fell. "You found them?"

Oscar nodded, expression as serious as Seb had ever seen it. "It had to be malicious." He must've seen Seb's confusion and curiosity. "We've been missing twenty head from the herd that had been grazing up in the mountain pasture. I found them today. Someone drove them off the edge of a cliff into that horseshoe-shaped canyon."

What? Seb's gut twisted uncomfortably at the unexpected mention of such violence.

"You sure someone killed them?" Jonas asked quietly.

"They wouldn't have walked off it without some prodding."

Jonas rubbed a hand over his face. Seb knew his father grieved the lost animals. Who would do such a thing?

"How long has this been going on? What did Matty say?" Seb asked. His mind whirled with questions.

"The cattle came up missing last week," Oscar said. "I only found the bodies today. Any sign of tracks are long gone."

Who would do something like that? And why? As far as Seb knew, Jonas had never had any enemies. He was an upstanding citizen, well-liked and respected. And Seb's brothers were the same. One of his brothers was a sheriff's deputy, for crying out loud. And Maxwell had served the community as a doctor for years. Could it have anything to do with the man who'd been terrorizing Cora Beth?

None of it made any sense.

"I don't like it," Jonas said. "But maybe we'd better pull the cattle down to graze in the lower pastures, where we can keep a better eye on them."

"There's not enough grass to last the summer," Oscar said. "And with our losses from last year, they need all the forage they can get."

So there had been losses, and he hadn't been there to help.

"I'm home now." Seb cleared his throat. "If I need to stay in the winter cabin and keep guard over them, I will."

Jonas looked surprised. "We weren't sure if you were staying."

Seb's face flushed with shame. He knew he deserved

that. He'd left when his family had needed everyone to keep the place running.

"I'm home for good," he said. "If you'll have me back."

Oscar wrinkled his nose. "You've lost your scrawniness, at least. We might have to test and see if you've got any work ethic left."

Jonas shook his head, a smile playing on his mouth. "We are mighty glad to have you back, son."

Seb was going to prove to all of them that he could be a real part of the family again.

13

For the first time, Emma hesitated outside the hotel dining room. Nerves were rattling through her because of Fran's words the night before. *I've seen the way he looks at you.*

Phillip had never shown any hint of feelings other than friendship toward her. They'd worked together for two years now, and he'd never made any overtures toward her.

She was being silly. Fran didn't know what she was talking about.

She entered the dining room and heard Phillip call out. "Emma, over here."

She'd told him earlier in the week that he didn't need to announce where he was sitting, not when they occupied the same table every day. It hadn't stopped him from calling out for her every morning when she arrived. She heard the rustle of his clothing as he moved around the table and helped her into her seat.

"There's tea and sugar on the table, just like you like it."

Today, his solicitousness felt cloying. Was it because of Fran's silliness?

They were close to the end of the book, and she didn't waste any time getting to work. They would have a session today and another tomorrow, and that should be it.

She was glad that during her last contract negotiation, Daniel had negotiated a stipend for her typist. She hadn't expected her books to be so popular. And having a brother who could negotiate a contract in her favor, that was another blessing.

She talked, he typed, while two hours passed. She sipped her tea after they'd finished. Her throat felt raw from the constant talking.

She liked the story. Liked the plucky heroine who had gotten herself into a load of trouble with a gang of stage-coach robbers. Tonight, she would work out the last little bit, and tomorrow she'd set the heroine free. Maybe she should have the feisty seamstress save the cowboy who had ridden to her rescue.

She could hear Phillip putting his typewriter in the heavy leather box that he used to keep it from being damaged as he carted it around. The sound stopped, and he sat back down across from her. His knee must've bumped the table, because the dishes rattled.

"Emma, there's something else I've been wanting to talk to you about."

She settled her teacup back in at saucer, using her

fingertips to guide the cup gently to its resting place. She turned her face in his direction.

He cleared his throat. "We've been working together for a while. And we've come to know each other rather well. My admiration for you has grown so that I can barely contain it."

Heat flooded her face, pulsing at the place where her jaw met her ear. What was he trying to say?

"I know you wanted to return to Wyoming. But I'm hoping I can convince you to come back to Denver with me. To be my wife."

A tiny laugh burbled out of her, and she shook herself. "I'm sorry." She hadn't meant to offend him. "I'm just—very surprised."

"It's all right." His tone was too high, and he cleared his throat, lowered his voice. "I wasn't sure—that is, I know I haven't made my feelings clear before this moment."

"I can't... As you said, I haven't even had a chance to settle in Wyoming yet." She didn't know what to say. Phillip was kind, but she didn't have deeper feelings for him, not like he claimed to have for her.

"I'm sure it must be a lot to think about. You should talk to your sister."

Emma knew her own mind. She took advice from Fran when she needed it, but she was perfectly capable of deciding this.

"Maybe you could give me an answer tomorrow, when we meet again."

Relieved that she didn't have to break his heart this instant, but mostly that she didn't have to ruin her final day of working with Phillip—getting the most important part of her manuscript on paper—she stood a little too quickly.

He accompanied her past the front desk and out onto the boardwalk. Yesterday, it had been Susie and Velma sent to town to fetch her, but today it was an unexpected voice that called out to her.

"Emma." That was Seb.

She felt Phillip bristle. Did he remember seeing Seb in Daniel's home back in Denver? He must.

"It's Phillip, isn't it?" Seb said.

She heard boot steps on the boardwalk and then felt Seb come close, his arm brushing hers as he must've reached out toward Phillip. She heard the slide of their skin as they shook hands.

"Seb White. I'm here to fetch Emma home."

There was a silence that stretched a little too long. What were they doing? Just staring at each other? Were they still shaking hands?

The moment was broken, and Seb's hand slipped beneath her elbow. "The wagon is just across the street."

Phillip called out after her. "Until tomorrow."

She lifted a hand to wave over her shoulder.

Seb was silent as they crossed the street.

She heard a horse's whicker, and Seb drew her to a stop.

"I should've asked—do you need to stop anywhere else before we head home?"

She spared a single thought for the beautiful shawl. Not today. "I'm ready."

He took her waist in her hands, and her breath caught in her throat as he assisted her over the wagon wheel and onto the seat.

She heard his footsteps as he crossed behind the wagon and then felt the shift as he levered himself onto the bench beside her.

"I was expecting Susie." Her voice sounded breathless to her own ears. Would he hear it too?

If he did, he didn't comment. "I was already coming into town. It's no trouble."

No trouble. He hadn't come because he'd wanted to see her or to have a chance to talk to her. He just happened to be in town.

She heard this soft catch of his breath. "I was happy to do it."

Her heart leaped.

SEB HAD BEEN ANTICIPATING this moment since he'd realized that he would be accompanying Emma home. Alone.

He and Oscar had ridden with Cora Beth to her farm, where they'd loaded up the chickens. There, Oscar had headed back to the homestead, and Seb had delivered Cora Beth to the train station and seen her safely off.

Oscar had been the one who'd mentioned needing to

find someone to bring Emma home from Bear Creek. Seb had jumped at the chance.

Right up until he'd seen her emerge from the hotel with her beau from back in Denver.

Phillip had hovered over her with a proprietary glint in his eyes. And then there'd been a sizing up as he'd shaken Seb's hand like he was trying to smash an egg in his grip.

Back in Denver, Emma had said she only worked with Phillip. That their relationship was not romantic.

But Wyoming was a long way to travel to work as a typist. Had things changed? Did the man have a claim on Emma?

Why else would he come so far?

He felt sick to his stomach. Emma had every right to move on. It had been a wild hope that she would be unattached when he was finally free.

"It will be nice to have a chance to catch up," Emma said softly.

The wagon jostled over a rut in the road, and she slid so that her hip bumped into his.

It was torture having her so close, not knowing where they stood.

"I'm sorry we didn't get a chance to talk yesterday," he said.

"I understood. Your family has missed you." But had she missed him? "And you had Cora Beth to look after."

She sat beside him, perfectly poised. Had he imagined the questioning tone in her voice? Was there a hint of jealousy?

Maybe he was projecting his feelings onto her.

"Cora Beth is an old friend from our school days. She needed some help, and I was there. I just dropped her off at the train station. She's going to visit her aunt for a while."

Emma's chin dipped slightly, her face tilting slightly toward him. "So she's not... You're not..."

She was curious! He latched on to her awkward statement like a fish onto a worm. "She and I are just friends. Always have been."

Color appeared high in her cheeks, and he was glad for it. He was opening his mouth to ask about Phillip when she spoke again.

"How have you been these past months? I thought about you. Wondered whether you were all right."

"Once I made it through the hard part, I came straight home. Being with you—and Daniel—made me remember. Made me want to come back here."

Her nose wrinkled. "You didn't really answer my question."

She was too intuitive. Of course she'd noticed.

How could he tell her about those dark days locked in a prison cell? He'd deserved every one of them. Deserved even more than he'd gotten. But if she knew about prison, he'd have to tell her about what had come before. He'd never told her about Tolliver, about being an enforcer and the awful things he'd done. As far as she knew, he was still one of the good guys.

And if that rosy blush was for him, he didn't want to

see the light dim from her eyes. Didn't want to see her admiration fade away.

"There were hard days. But that's over now." He could only hope that would be enough. What he needed to know was whether she'd missed him.

He didn't know how to navigate the tenuous connection between them.

"Are you and Phillip a couple?" He choked out the last words, envy nearly blinding him.

She flushed again, this time pressing her hand to her cheeks.

"What?" he asked. "I saw him once, in Denver. Had a feeling maybe he wanted to be more than friends."

She shook her head, still with her hands at her cheeks. "Was it obvious to everyone except me?"

What did that mean?

"Phillip asked me to marry him."

Shock and dismay rattled him down to his toes. Emma was engaged. To Phillip.

The news felt like a cinch clamping around his chest.

Of course. Of course she was taken.

She was beautiful, kind, independent, and she had a lovely spirit. If only he'd made different choices.

He tried to form words to congratulate her, but his tongue was twisted and wrong.

And then he caught sight of a rider coming their way and fast.

He touched Emma's wrist. She jumped.

"Someone's riding this way from the homestead."

As the rider neared, he saw two smaller forms in the saddle. Walt, with Andrew clinging to his brother riding double. He reined in the horses, drawing the wagon to a halt.

Walt pulled his horse to a stop in front of them. His animal was already winded.

"What's going on?" Seb demanded.

Walt panted. "We're heading to town to fetch Maxwell. Matty's real bad hurt."

"He musta got into a fight or something," Andrew chimed in. "He's all busted up."

Emma pressed one hand to her mouth. "Oh no."

"We gotta hurry," Walt said.

Seb waved the boys on, calling, "Be safe!" after them.

He slapped the reins. "Giddup."

Urgency nipped at his heels, though he wouldn't be any more help than his Ma and Sarah at doctoring up his brother. But he needed to see Matty. To know he was all right.

It must be bad if his family had sent for Maxwell. His parents had had plenty of practice patching up a house full of rough-and-tumble boys over the years.

Seb knew that Matty sometimes rode into danger in his job as a deputy, but up until now he'd never been badly hurt.

Seb forgot all about Emma and her fiancé as he pushed the horses as fast as he could toward home.

When they arrived, Emma begged to be let off at Fran

and Edgar's cabin. "If I go up to the main house, I'll just be in the way."

He hated that she felt that way but knew that there was a good chance his brother was surrounded by folks already.

He helped her clamber out of the wagon and drove the horses to the barn, where he unhitched them. He made sure they were fed and watered.

In the kitchen he found Sarah and her middle daughter, Susie, boiling water and looking worried. They must've known it was too soon for Maxwell to walk through the door, but the tiny amount of hope in their expressions dimmed when they saw him.

"What happened?" he asked.

Susie had tears in her eyes.

It was Sarah who answered. "We don't know. He was unconscious when he arrived. Someone had slung him over his saddle face down and tied him on."

"After they beat the snot out of him," Susie added. "He was black and blue, bleeding from his head."

"Susie. That's not helpful."

Sarah urged her daughter to check with Penny and Catherine, Matty's wife, to see if they needed anything. Susie carried some clean towels down the hall with her.

"What can I do?"

Sarah looked as helpless as he felt. "Your mother has bandaged him up the best she can. We're waiting on Maxwell."

Seb wondered whether he should ride into town to the

sheriff's office. Maybe if he could find out who or what Matty had been after, he could figure out what had happened to his brother.

But before he could decide whether to go or not, Jonas appeared from the back hallway, looking haggard. "His breathing is shallow. I don't know what else we can do for him. Only pray."

14

Thunk.

T hunk. Seb stacked another half log on the chopping block and swung the ax again.

Thunk.

Matty hadn't roused during the night. It was coming on to mid-morning, and Seb was working out his frustration by chopping wood. His muscles burned, reminding him that he hadn't done this kind of physical labor in far too long.

Earlier he'd seen Emma and Susie load up in the wagon and head for town. No doubt Emma was glad to escape the dreary cloud hanging over the entire family. Maybe her beau would comfort her.

Seb swung the ax again.

Thunk.

It didn't help.

He was angry that he couldn't do anything for his brother.

And angry that he'd missed his chance with Emma.

Maybe they'd never had one.

Thunk.

Angry. Frustrated. Sad.

Would she leave Wyoming now? She must've come to visit Fran and Eloise and Henry. But if she was getting married, surely she would return to Denver.

Maybe it had been a mistake to come home. Misfortune seemed to be falling on everyone, and he couldn't help feeling as if he'd brought it with him.

That was ridiculous, wasn't it?

The stack of logs had dwindled, and he finished the last few pieces, grateful to be done with the chore. Maybe there were stalls to muck out in the barn.

He couldn't sit around and do nothing.

Waiting to find out if his brother would wake up again was pure torture.

Maxwell had examined Matty last night, noting bruising in his midsection and ribs, like he'd been bludgeoned. There'd been no swelling that might signify internal injuries, which was a blessing.

The head wound was trickier. Maxwell had found a huge lump swollen at Matty's hairline behind one ear. Someone had used a lot of force to knock Matty out.

Seb had stood out in the hall, shoulder-to-shoulder with Edgar and Oscar and Davy, while Maxwell examined their brother. Matty's wife Catherine had been sitting at his side, and Seb had heard her soft sobs as Maxwell explained just how bad the injuries were.

If Matty didn't wake up... It didn't bear thinking about.

Seb had been gone for long enough that he didn't know which chore was most important to complete next. He headed to the main house, where Oscar had been sitting with Jonas in the kitchen.

He found the kitchen a hive of activity.

Penny was pulling together what looked like a pot of soup. He'd seen her slide a huge ham into the oven earlier in the day. Had she changed her mind about what she was cooking for the noon meal?

Sarah was watching over Velma, Walt, Ida, and Andrew at the table. The four children had their schoolwork open on the table in front of them, but they weren't working so much as whispering amongst themselves.

If he wasn't mistaken, those were tears on Penny's cheeks. Sarah's cheeks were pink and her eyes bright.

He hung his hat on a peg by the door. "Is Oscar around?"

Oscar would know what needed to be done next. Seb wouldn't bother Pa right now.

Penny swiped at her cheek briskly, glancing over her shoulder. "He's back with Matty. Your brother woke up."

Matty was awake?

Seb kissed his ma on the cheek. A fresh hope made his steps light as he went down the hall to see for himself. Pa was heading toward him in the narrow hallway, and Seb felt a moment of dread when he spotted Jonas's dark frown.

What was going on? Had Matty slipped back into unconsciousness? Ma and Sarah had been lit up with hope a few moments ago. They would be devastated.

Jonas put up a hand to stop Seb in the hallway.

"What happened?" Seb asked.

"It's best to hear from your brother, but he's very weak." Jonas was trying to convey something with his expression, his eyes fierce and focused. "I don't want you getting your brother riled up. Once he says what he's got to say, you come back out, and we'll talk, you and I."

With those ominous words ringing in his ears, Seb pushed past his father into Matty's bedroom.

Catherine was still at Matty's side, holding his hand. The room was mostly dark, curtains drawn against the sunlight.

His brother lay flat on his back.

Seb remembered those few days back in Denver when he'd suffered from the concussion Tolliver's goons had given him. How the bright light had made him feel as if his head were going to explode.

Oscar stood in the corner, his arms crossed over his chest.

"Seb?" Matty's voice was weaker than Seb had ever heard it.

He moved to stand at the side of the bed. "I'm right here."

Matty swallowed, the movement difficult.

Seb hadn't wanted to be in the way last night and he hadn't seen his brother up close until now. He had cuts and bruises covering his face, even on his shoulders visible above the blanket. His right eye had been blackened. And there were still traces of dried blood crusted around his nose. Each breath he drew rasped and rattled in his chest.

Matty spoke with difficulty. "He said... that I... was the message."

Matty's words didn't make any sense.

"Who did this to you?" Seb asked.

Catherine glared at him. Had he barked the words instead of a whisper as he'd meant to? Seeing his brother like this made every protective instinct inside him roar like a mama bear with a threatened cub.

"Said his name was Tolliver."

Seb froze. Every muscle coiled. The little bit of air in his chest lodged, and he couldn't breathe.

It couldn't be.

Matty wasn't finished. "He said he was sending you a message. ... I'm the message."

No. "I'm—so sorry." His voice broke on the words. "This is all my fault."

Oscar moved in the corner, and Seb shook loose of the icy bonds that had frozen his limbs. He wanted to squeeze his brother's shoulder but was afraid of hurting the man further, so he settled for a gentle pat on Matty's hand, the only visible part of him that looked unharmed. "You just rest up."

He left the room blindly, Oscar on his heels.

His mind was reeling. When everything had gone down in Colorado, Tolliver's criminal enterprise had been dismantled, but the man himself had escaped.

And somehow ended up here, where he'd sent Seb a message by nearly killing his brother.

Jonas was waiting in the family room, arms crossed and face expressionless. Oscar came in close behind Seb, and it was so much like being herded around the way he'd experienced with the prison guards that for a moment he forgot where he was.

"You want to tell me what's chasing you, son?" Jonas sent a glance to the kitchen.

Seb was conscious of the children. If they kept their voices low enough, they wouldn't be overheard.

Seb shook his head, still trying to wrap his mind around what Matty had said and what it meant. "I didn't think anyone had followed me home."

"Well, that ain't the case. Obviously," Oscar interjected.

Jonas waved him off. "Let him speak."

Seb turned away. He rubbed his hands down his face and back up to push them into his hair.

"I fell in with some unfriendly folk down in Denver. If one of them followed me here—"

"And tracked down your family?" Oscar guessed.

"I don't know how he got the jump on Matty." Seb's brother was one of the best lawmen around. He was sharp as the point of a nail, too smart to ride into an ambush. "We need to keep everybody close." He inhaled sharply as he remembered Emma and Susie riding off in a wagon toward town hours ago.

Back in Denver, Beckett—Tolliver's right-hand man— had seen Emma's face. She could be in danger this very minute.

"Susie and Emma went to town by themselves earlier." He headed for the door.

Jonas extended his arm, stopping Seb. "Surely whoever did this wouldn't hurt a young woman."

Seb scowled. "You don't know him. And you don't want to." Seb ran for the door.

Oscar followed him. "I'll go with you."

Seb shook his head. "It's me he wants."

"All the more reason why you should have someone to watch your back."

Seb stole a moment to look at Sarah and Oscar's two youngest, sitting at the table. "You've got people who need you here. I'm good." He slammed the door in his brother's face.

His hands were shaking as he rushed to saddle a gelding in the barn. If Tolliver touched one hair on Emma's head...

But Seb was hours behind the girls. Even if he killed his horse in a wild gallop, he might be too late.

EMMA HEARD the cracking of the keys as Phillip finished typing the last sentence of her manuscript. She heard the funny squawk when he pulled the paper from the machine, the tiny flutter as the paper landed on the stack of others lying between them on the table. Phillip had brought the entire manuscript today, and she'd flipped the pages through her fingers earlier.

They were finished.

When they had met that morning, she had asked him if they could jump right into their work and talk afterward. He'd agreed.

And now *afterward* was here. And she was going to have to let him down.

She heard Susie's voice from the hotel lobby. Otherwise, it seemed the dining room was empty. There were sounds of cooking and low voices from the kitchen, but she and Phillip were alone. He boxed up his typewriter, giving her another few moments of reprieve.

And then he cleared his throat. "I realize that after what happened with your sister's family last night, the timing of this conversation isn't ideal."

She held her breath. Maybe he was going to let her off the hook.

"But I do have to catch a train this afternoon."

Ah. He still wanted an answer.

"Phillip, I—"

"You've been a bundle of nerves all morning," he said. "As you aren't fluttering with joy, I think I can guess your answer to my proposal."

She'd hardly slept a wink at all the night before. Partly from worrying about Matty and his injuries, but there'd also been many thoughts about this moment.

She braced for his hurt to spill over as anger. That was why she'd asked Susie to come inside. To watch over her.

"I'm sorry. I just don't feel the same way. I think of you as a friend, a dear friend."

There was an awkward pause.

"Of course I wish things could've been different," he said, "but I understand."

His voice was tight. She wanted to reach out to him in comfort but was afraid he might take it the wrong way.

"Should I look for someone else to work with me on my next book?" she asked tentatively.

"I'll be devastated if you do. I can't wait to find out what kind of trouble you get your next character into."

In the past they had celebrated finishing each manuscript by sharing a meal, but this time Phillip begged off.

Emma couldn't blame him.

She wasn't hungry either. She just wanted to return to the homestead and find out if there'd been any change in Matty's condition.

She was standing up to fetch Susie, who was flirting with the front desk clerk, when awareness raised goosebumps on her arms. Someone slid into Phillip's now-vacant chair.

"Hello, Emma."

. . .

SEB MUST HAVE LOOKED like a crazy person as he rode into town like his rear end was on fire. He knew Emma would be at the hotel. Would Susie be with her?

He saw Emma's bright hair in the front window that opened up to the boardwalk. Relief sliced through him, visceral and powerful. If her fiancé was still around, he would tell the man to get her on a train back to Colorado. If Tolliver was in Wyoming, Colorado should be safe enough.

But as he drew up at the hitching post, he couldn't quite make out the figure sitting across from her at the table.

The man's seat was angled behind the window frame. To Seb's consternation, he couldn't make out that stupid derby hat that Phillip had worn yesterday.

Was that...?

Fear grabbed him by the throat, and he leaped off his horse, bolting for the hotel's front door. By the time he got inside, Emma and Susie were emerging from the dining room, arm-in-arm. Emma clutched a sheaf of paper to her midsection.

"Who was that?" he demanded.

Emma's head came up at his strident question.

It was Susie who answered, an ornery smile crossing her lips. "Emma, honey, don't tell him anything. You don't have to air your private business to Seb or any of his brothers." Susie grinned at him. "Emma can have as many suitors as she wants."

He didn't have time for Susie's nonsense. "That wasn't Phillip," he said to Emma.

Her forehead pinched as if he was speaking a foreign language and she was trying to understand him. "It was not, in fact."

"Who was it?"

Out of the two young women, Emma seemed to grasp his urgency. "Mr. Richards is a surveyor. He's been in town for several weeks. He's not a suitor."

Susie smirked.

Seb ignored her.

He'd only had a glimpse of the man's profile through the window. He could've sworn it had been Tolliver sitting across from Emma at that table. What if he'd used an alias?

"Where did he go?"

"Didn't he come out the front door?" Susie asked.

No one had exited as he'd been running into the hotel. If the man had left a few moments before Emma, he should've been in sight where they stood in the hotel lobby.

Seb's eyes lit on the wide staircase that took up half of the space.

"I'm going to see if he went upstairs."

If this Richards was a real surveyor, he might have a room at the hotel. If he was who he said he was, then Tolliver was still out there.

Seb leveled a look at Susie. "Matty came to." There wasn't time to tell the whole story, nor was this the place.

"There's danger, and I want you to stand right here until I come back. Do not move."

He could only hope that Emma would listen if Susie refused to wait.

He ran up the stairs. The hallway ran both directions. To the right was a dead end. Empty.

To the left, the hallway made a turn. Seb thought he saw a flash of clothing disappear around the corner.

He hurried in that direction.

He rounded the bend, walked smack into...

A fist.

Seb was shoved up against the wall.

Tolliver pressed a forearm against his throat, cutting off his air supply. The older man had been a fighter in his day, and he knew just how to stand to keep Seb from gaining any leverage that he could use to get loose.

That didn't stop Seb from landing a punch to Tolliver's ribs. Tolliver didn't even grunt.

"So you finally made it back home."

Seb tried to shove the other man away, but he was trapped. He couldn't move.

"It was sheer chance that I remembered the name of your hometown. Such a quaint little place. It wasn't even on the map."

Tolliver's forearm pressed into his windpipe, and Seb gasped for breath.

Tolliver sneered. "It's been a pleasure getting to know the folks around here. Including your family."

Seb couldn't breathe. His vision was starting to go dark at the edges. But that didn't stop him from struggling.

"Did you get my message?" Tolliver chuckled. "I wasn't certain whether he would survive to pass on my name, but I had some other ideas if he didn't."

Seb used the last of the air in his lungs to speak through clenched teeth. "Stay. Away. From. My. Family."

Tolliver laughed.

"I don't think so. I could kill you right now." He used his eyes to gesture down to where his jacket had fallen open. He had a revolver strapped to his side. "But that wouldn't be enough."

Seb had known Tolliver was no good. But the pure evil now revealing itself in Tolliver's icy gaze was something altogether different.

Seb was afraid.

"You took everything from me," Tolliver said. "And I'm going to return the favor."

He let go just as Seb's brain was about to shut down from lack of oxygen.

Seb fell to his hands and knees, coughing and shaking as his lungs expanded. By the time he stood, Tolliver was nowhere to be seen.

Had he gone into one of the rooms?

No. There was another exit at the end of the hall, one that led to a stairway that descended into the alley behind the hotel. Or maybe he'd gone back down the front stairway.

Seb thought about Susie and Emma in the lobby, sitting ducks.

He ran down the stairs, still coughing and gagging through his bruised throat.

Susie was scanning the area, seeming bored, but when her eyes flicked up to the stairway and saw him, her entire demeanor changed. "What happened?"

Emma had been standing quietly beside her, but her head came swiftly up.

He coughed once more. "I'm all right." His voice rasped. "We need to get back to the homestead."

"I was hoping to stop at the post office to mail my manuscript," Emma said softly.

"The only place I'm comfortable with you going is straight to the train depot with your fiancé. It's too dangerous otherwise."

Emma's brow crinkled with confusion.

Susie snorted softly.

Emma's mouth moved. After a moment, she said, "I don't have a fiancé."

Susie was looking at him speculatively. "She turned him down."

His two sides were at war. *Joy.* She wasn't engaged to Phillip. *Terror.* If she stayed in Wyoming, she would be in danger.

"I'd still feel better if you got on the train and went with Phillip back to Daniel's place in Denver."

He saw from the stubborn light in her eyes that she

wouldn't heed his advice. "This is my home. I'm not running away."

Her word struck like a barb. And he was out of time to argue. He needed to get the girls home, where he was going to have to confess everything. He felt sick to his stomach just thinking about it.

But there was nothing to be done.

15

E veryone in the family was gathered at the picnic tables, waiting for Seb's announcement. Emma sat with her hands in her lap, relying on the little patience she could muster.

She hadn't been able to get a word out of Seb on the way home from town. He'd been silent, reminding her more of the hardened man she'd come to know in Denver than the young man she'd fallen for years past.

What was so important that he had to gather the whole family?

The children had been settled inside with Velma and Walt in charge. That might not last long.

Catherine remained inside at Matty's side. He'd been slipping in and out of consciousness. It was clear he wasn't out of the woods yet.

On their flight from town, Seb had thought to visit Maxwell and Hattie and asked them to come too. He'd insisted that it was an emergency, and they'd close the clinic, though they hadn't seemed happy about it.

Fran had suggested none-so-gently that Emma stay inside and help watch over the children.

But Seb had overheard and said, "Emma needs to stay. This involves her."

"What is going on?" Fran asked in a whisper.

Emma shrugged. She was as clueless as everyone else.

There were so many whispers and murmurs that Emma couldn't get a good idea of where everyone was sitting. There were just too many of them.

Finally, Seb cleared his throat from several feet away. By the sound of it, he was standing at the head of the table.

"After I left home, I needed a way to make money." His voice was still raspy, as it had been with the few words he'd uttered since he'd barreled down the hotel stairs. "I started boxing. If I fought a match every other week, I could earn enough cash to get by."

There was a surprised gasp—maybe from Penny—at the nearest picnic table.

"The places where I fought weren't—well, they were rough."

Emma had only heard of fights like those happening in saloons and gambling halls. Oh, Seb.

"By the time I got down to Denver, I'd gotten pretty good. After I won a few rounds handily, I was approached by a man I'd never met before. He wanted to sponsor me for several fights in a row. I would work for him. I would win, and he would pay me a nice salary. Provide lodging. Provide whatever I wanted."

He let out a sound of disgust. With himself? "I took the deal. But I lost the second fight. And then I lost the third. And my benefactor wanted to be repaid."

Fran gasped safely from beside Emma. "I can't imagine!"

Emma didn't have to imagine. She'd changed his bandages and felt the tremors as he'd worked to regain his strength. Was that what had happened?

"The way he wanted me to repay him... it wasn't pretty. At first, he had me threaten a few people who he claimed owed him money. There was nothing physical about it, just me knocking on their doors to collect. But then he expected more. He expected me to use my fists to get his money."

There was a long moment of silence.

Seb kept going. "I saw a lot of things. Bad things. I should've walked away, but by that time, I owed him, and I was so deep... I was ashamed of what I'd done and who I'd become.

"I thought I didn't have any morals left, but then Tolliver wanted me to collect from a woman and her ten-year-old boy. He told me to rough up the boy as much as I needed to in order to get the woman to pay."

Seb's voice was rough, as if he was holding off tears. "They didn't have the money. And I couldn't beat up a kid. I told my boss I was done. I don't know what I thought would happen at that point." His next words came muffled, as if he'd covered his mouth with his hand. "I intended to hop on a train and leave. I didn't know where. Anywhere but Denver. And then some thugs jumped me. I ended up beaten just as badly as Matty. Someone found me and dropped me off on Daniel's doorstep."

Emma's face flamed as she felt eyes on her. Everyone knew she'd lived with Daniel in Denver. Were they angry that she hadn't mentioned seeing Seb?

"Daniel and Emma helped me get back on my feet, but before I could leave town, I was attacked again. *We* were attacked. Emma was there."

Fran clutched Emma's hand.

"This time I took care of the two guys."

Emma would never forget the violent sounds of Seb fighting those two men. The fear that had stuck in her throat when she'd worried he hadn't been the one left standing.

"I was..." Here, he stumbled, took a moment before continuing. "The last thing I wanted was for somebody to hurt Emma or Daniel because of me. Daniel helped me go to the US Marshals, and I was there through the winter, helping the law bring down Tolliver's organization. When it was all said and done, he escaped."

"It's summer now," Jonas said. "Why didn't you come home...?"

Emma hadn't even noticed the discrepancy. She was still trying to understand how someone like Seb had worked for someone as evil as the man he described. Why hadn't he told her in Denver? Had he been afraid she wouldn't understand?

There was a beat of silence. "Part of the deal was that I serve six months in prison."

Someone gasped, and this time Emma was sure it had been Penny.

"It wasn't so bad," he reassured his mother.

But Emma could only imagine the horrors he must have faced. And he'd done it all alone. Why hadn't he told her? She could've written him letters...

It came to her quickly. He'd been ashamed.

He wasn't done. "Tolliver is here. He's the one who hurt Matty. He's been using an alias. You know him as Richards."

The knowledge moved through Emma with a shudder. The man she'd sat across from in the hotel dining room today was the man that had tried to kill Seb? The same one who had nearly killed Matty?

There were more murmurs.

"Believe me," Seb said. "He can make himself seem normal. Even seem like a prince. But underneath, he's a snake. He doesn't have any mercy inside him. I saw him in town today. He could've killed me, but he said he's after everyone I love."

There were no murmurs now, only stunned silence.

"If the US Marshals want him, why don't they come up here?" That was Oscar.

"We should talk to the sheriff. See if he can wire them." Even the usually unflappable Jonas seemed shaken.

"Yes," Seb said. "But Tolliver is slippery. He could escape by the time they arrived. Or hide out somewhere."

"We can protect ourselves," Edgar muttered his agreement from the other side of Fran.

"We've got to be careful," Jonas cautioned. "We can't let him pick us off one by one."

"Somehow he got the jump on Matty," Maxwell reminded everyone.

"We can't just wait around..." Davy said quietly.

What peace had reigned was over gone as the brother started arguing about what to do next and the women whispered worries to one another.

Emma was too stunned to move.

SEB FELT as if he had the flu. His head felt hot and his hands felt cold.

He'd done it. He'd confessed his sins to his family.

But he didn't feel absolved.

Jonas had kept his reaction carefully hidden, his face impassive. Penny's eyes were filled with tears. She'd started crying in earnest when he'd mentioned prison.

Maxwell hadn't been able to hide his surprise. Oscar's jaw was still clenched.

His brothers had the right to be angry. He'd kept this from all of them. Matty had been hurt because of him.

He felt like he was going to throw up.

His brothers were huddling up over to one side of the picnic tables, arguing over tactics. He picked up snatches.

We should go after this guy!

We need to have a watch overnight.

Someone's gotta alert the sheriff.

Nobody's going anywhere alone.

And Emma.

Emma sat quietly next to Fran, just as she had throughout his explanation. Her face was pale in the falling dusk.

No matter that he'd tried to keep his gaze away from her, he hadn't been able to stop glancing at her as he spoke.

Did she hate him now?

He didn't care if his brothers would tease him later. He had something he needed to say.

He strode to where she sat next to her sister. "Emma, can I talk to you?"

Fran looked at him speculatively. He couldn't quite meet her gaze.

Fran stopped Emma from standing with a hand to her arm. "I'm sure you can say whatever you want to say to Emma in front of both of us."

"I really can't."

Emma pressed her sister's hand. "It's all right."

She stood and reached for the walking stick he had seen her use often. He was surprised when she reached out the other hand to him. It seemed natural for him to tuck her in close to his side.

But right now, he didn't know which way was up. His entire life felt turned inside out. He'd paid his debt. He was supposed to be free from this mess.

He didn't dare take her far. Not with all of his brothers watching. There was a tall maple a dozen yards from the house, and he drew her with him to stand beneath it. He took her left hand in his left and unwrapped it from his arm, then placed her palm against the tree to orient her. He stepped away.

"Why didn't you tell me, in Denver?" she asked quietly. "Daniel knew, didn't he?"

Her face was turned toward him, but her eyes seemed focused somewhere over his shoulder. Everything he wanted to say was so jumbled up inside of him. He'd wanted to protect her from his past. But really, he'd wanted to protect himself. Wanted her to believe he was still the upstanding guy she'd left behind.

Shame heated his neck.

She laughed a wobbly laugh and dashed a tear from her cheek. "I'm being unfair, aren't I? After I kept my blindness from you."

"It's not the same." His voice emerged rough, his emotions getting the better of him.

Over Emma's shoulder, he saw Fran get up from the table and approach Edgar, drawing him away from Oscar and Maxwell and Davy. They looked toward where Seb and Emma spoke.

He was short on time.

"I'm sorry," he said. "For everything. I can never make amends to all the people I've hurt, the people I stole from in Tolliver's name. I don't expect any kind of forgiveness. I don't deserve it. I never wanted you to find out because I'd hoped that after I got out, I could work hard and make myself worthy."

He'd thought he would have more time.

Emma's head turned to the side. Seb looked past her to see Edgar approaching. She must've heard his steps in the grass.

Seb lowered his voice. "I never stopped caring about you."

Edgar cleared his throat. "This isn't the time, Seb. We need you to answer some questions about Tolliver."

He saw the truth in Edgar's face. Now wasn't the time to declare himself to Emma. And there wasn't going to be a time. His brother looked concerned, almost angry.

That cinch around Seb's chest wrapped tighter. He had betrayed his family's trust. None of them would ever look at him the same again.

And the worst part was, he deserved it.

Emma's face was still drawn. He couldn't decipher her expression.

Edgar cleared his throat. "Emma, Fran needs your help to settle the little ones. Let's go."

He watched her walk away on Edgar's arm, knowing that nothing was ever going to be the same again.

"What was that?" Fran asked. Her tone was impatient as Emma approached.

There were little groups of conversation going on all around, and it was hard for Emma to focus.

She was still reeling from what Seb had told her. He cared about her. He'd been coming to find her.

She didn't have a chance to answer her sister as Velma rushed up with Eloise in her arms. "Here's mama."

"Mama!" The child's high, sweet voice rang out.

"Thank you, Velma." Fabric shifted, more movement. "Thanks for keeping them."

Velma's footsteps darted off.

"What is going on?" Fran asked. The baby was fussing, Eloise's voice calling *mama* from the ground, but Fran ignored the children. "What did Seb want?"

Emma heard the judgment in her sister's voice. Fran wouldn't easily forgive that Seb had put Emma in danger.

Maybe it was time to come clean. She sighed, hoped nobody but her sister would hear when she lowered her voice and said, "I've been in love with Seb for years. Since I was sixteen." It had happened quietly, creeping up on her a little at a time as she'd settled into life on the ranch. The first time she'd realized it was happening had been a few days after her sixteenth birthday. She had walked outside of the ranch house and seen him horsing around with his younger sister Breanna. And she'd been enchanted.

Fran made a noise of disbelief.

"He asked to come courting when I turned eighteen. Everything was just beginning... And then I lost my sight." She swallowed hard. "I shouldn't have left."

Fran's voice was icy when she responded. "You leaving has nothing to do with the mess he's gotten himself into."

Maybe not. But it'd been the catalyst for everything that had happened since.

"I think it's time we went back to the cabin. Edgar will let us know when the men are ready to take action."

Emma shook her head. "I'm staying to help Penny."

"No." Fran took Emma's wrist.

Emma gently disengaged herself. "When I arrived on your doorstep, I told you that I aim to live my life with more freedom than what I experienced living with Daniel."

"It's not about that. I know you're perfectly capable."

She made an expression that she hoped conveyed her skepticism.

"You loved the Seb that you knew five years ago. That Seb would never have joined ranks with a criminal." One of the nearby conversations—Cecilia and Sara, she thought—went hushed at Fran's harsh words.

Had Seb expected this kind of judgment from his family? Was that why he'd refused to ask for help back in Denver?

She could hear low voices from where the men were congregated several yards away. Within their circle, was there tension like this? Did any of Seb's brothers wear distress or disgust in their expressions? She wanted to know so badly and cursed the fact that she couldn't see.

"Seb has changed. But I have, too. I'm going to help Penny."

Emma stepped away wondering what expression her

sister wore. She used her cane and followed the sound of Penny's voice as the other woman moved into the farmhouse, the door closing and cutting off what she was saying.

Emma followed at her own pace. Her prickly scalp told her that at least one person was watching her. Maybe Fran. Maybe everyone.

It didn't matter what Seb's family thought right now. He needed every ally. And she was going to stand beside him the way she hadn't back in Colorado.

She found the door and opened it.

Penny was in the kitchen, speaking in low voices with Ida. When Emma entered, their conversation stopped.

A blush rose in Emma's cheeks, but she held her own. "I'd like to help. What do you need?"

16

Seb rode into town with his father to escort Maxwell and Hattie back to their clinic. The pair felt sure that they had enough friends in town to look out for them that they wouldn't be in too much danger.

Seb wished he could be as sure, but anxiety ate up his belly from the inside out.

Maxwell helped Hattie out of their buggy, and she waited on the boardwalk while Maxwell turned to Seb still in the saddle.

"Can you come down for a minute? I need to say something to you."

Jonas didn't bat an eye. "I'll walk through the clinic with Hattie and make sure everything looks secure."

The two disappeared inside. Seb dismounted and tied his horse to the hitching post.

The streets were quiet this time of afternoon, only a

couple of wagons in front of the mercantile and one horse in front of the bank.

Seb looked curiously at his older brother. Maxwell was one of the kindest, most patient men Seb knew. He was agitated now. His feet shifted nervously. Was he going to reprimand Seb for bringing this trouble to their door?

Maxwell took off his hat and sighed. "I didn't realize that... well, I didn't think anything of it when Emma asked me to keep her blindness a secret."

Oh.

It wasn't about Tolliver at all. It was about Emma.

Seb had known that his brothers were too perceptive. He just hadn't expected Maxwell to be the first to say something about it.

"I didn't know—"

"No one did." Seb swept his hat off his head and beat it against his thigh, sending up a puff of dust. "I wanted some time to woo her without all my stinkin' brothers making jokes at our expense."

"Still—"

"She was scared. Didn't know how things were going to turn out." Like he was now. He couldn't see a way out of this that turned out for the good.

"Maybe not." Maxwell held his eye contact. "But maybe if I'd known that it mattered—that *she* mattered—I could've talked you out of leaving town."

Seb shook his head. "No one could've out-stubborned me. I was determined to go."

But the fact that Maxwell cared now meant a lot.

"For what it's worth, I'm sorry," Seb said. "About all this..."

Maxwell embraced him, which gave Seb a few seconds to blink the hot wetness from his eyes.

Jonas walked out of the clinic. "Everything's been locked up tight."

Maxwell let him go and embraced his father, too, and then left Seb and Jonas to do what they'd come to town to do.

They visited the sheriff's office first.

Seb didn't recognize the man behind the desk with the tin star pinned to his chest. But Matty had said they could trust sheriff Everly, that he was an honorable man who couldn't be bought by Tolliver.

They stood inside the sparsely furnished office, and Jonas left it to Seb to explain. He couldn't help but be aware of the three empty cells just beyond a doorway behind the sheriff's desk. The sight of the iron bars soured his stomach as memories fought to get free.

He forced himself to focus.

The sheriff had already heard about Matty's injuries. But this was the first he'd heard of a message being sent to the White family.

Seb told him about the threats Tolliver had made in the hotel. And about everything that had happened back in Colorado. He even had a wanted poster that the US Marshals had made up, which he handed over.

The sheriff listened intently and then sat with his

hands folded on his desk. "Those are some very grave accusations you're making, son."

Seb couldn't read him. "If you contact the US Marshals' office in Denver, they'll tell you about their case against Tolliver."

"You sure the person who assaulted you at the hotel is the same guy?" He glanced down at the poster.

Seb would never forget the evil in Tolliver's eyes. "I'm certain."

The sheriff shook his head. "With Matty out of commission, I'm short one deputy. I'll have my hands full keeping order in town as it is. I doubt I can spare anyone to watch over your place."

Jonas nodded. "We weren't expecting that."

"And if this Tolliver is his nasty as you claim he is, I'll need to make sure no one in my town gets swept up in this."

Seb's heart sank. He hadn't expected the sheriff to roll out the welcome wagon for him, not with his history. But he had hoped Everly would give them more help than this. His family was only six men strong. How could they protect all the women and children—and themselves—for more than a few days?

They shook the sheriff's hand and took their leave.

At the hotel, the desk clerk showed them the guest register. There was no one named Tolliver or Richards listed. The man behind the counter didn't know anyone matching the description Seb gave.

That was a dead end.

"Let's go talk to Mabel over at the general store," Jonas suggested as they stepped out onto the boardwalk. "She knows everybody." And was the biggest gossip in town. "Maybe she'll know where Tolliver is staying."

Mabel was finishing up cutting fabric from a bolt and conversing quietly with a customer when they entered. She looked up, but the smile of greeting she wore faded when she registered who was standing inside her store. Her gaze flicked from Seb to Jonas and back again. Seb's heart sank.

It was only a matter of minutes before Mabel finished up with her customer. Jonas took off his hat and approached the counter. Seb followed.

"How can I help you today?" Seb was pretty sure he wasn't imagining the cool tone in her voice.

His throat was dry, and he was thankful when his pa spoke first.

"You know Seb's back in town."

Mabel nodded.

"He had a bit of trouble while he was away from home. and some of that trouble followed him here."

Mabel turned an assessing gaze on Seb, one that burned like acid as she narrowed her eyes. "I heard a little about the trouble you've been in. Prison, wasn't it?"

Seb reeled from the blow. The only people he'd told about where he'd been were his family and the sheriff. The only other person who could've breathed a word of it was Tolliver.

Apparently, Tolliver had been spreading stories.

He'd threaten to take everything that mattered to Seb. What better way to start than to taint Seb's reputation?

Mabel wasn't done. "I want to know why I didn't hear about this from your family. Seems mighty suspicious for you all to be keeping this a secret."

"Nothing suspicious about it," Jonas said. "Seb only came back to us a few days ago." His voice was as calm and unruffled as ever. Meanwhile, Seb felt as if he had been tumbled head over end.

"My family didn't know where I was," Seb interjected. "Or that I'd been in prison."

This was exactly the thing he'd wanted to spare his family from. Folks in town looking at them, judging them, because of what Seb had done. He felt sick to his stomach.

"Seb came home to make things right," Jones said. "He's my son and an important part of our family."

Now, Seb's inside swelled with emotion. That Jonas would still claim him after what he'd done, the trouble he was causing... He didn't deserve it. Inside, there was still a part of him—that abandoned little boy on the street, hungry and alone—who remembered that Jonas had rescued him. Jonas had provided love and connection and family. And now he was doing it all over again.

Unlike Seb, Mabel didn't seem moved. She was frowning. "Did y'all need something from the store today?"

"The man you know as Richards," Seb said quickly, "the man who told you about me? He's a bad character. In Denver, he robbed and blackmailed and sometimes even murdered."

Mabel's lips twisted. "Right. And you're so trustworthy."

How could he make her understand? "It's true I got myself into a bad situation. I take responsibility for my actions. But once I realized what he was capable of, I did everything I could to help the law bring him in. He's dangerous."

Jonas spoke. "You've known Seb since he was a little tyke. He's made some mistakes, but he's back home now. And you've known me for just as long. I trust my son when he says that this fellow is dangerous. His real name's Tolliver."

Mabel still looked unsure.

"You can see his wanted poster at the sheriff's office," Seb said. "Do you happen to know where he's staying?"

She shook her head. Her expression had turned hard. "If this man is the criminal you say he is—"

"He is. Ask the sheriff," Seb interrupted.

"You brought him here. It's on your head if we're all in danger."

Seb lost his breath. She was right. Of course she was right.

"If y'all aren't going to buy anything, I've got some books to do in the back." It was a clear dismissal, and they took their leave.

Whatever kernel of hope Seb had held onto that they would find help in town was rapidly dwindling.

They didn't quit, though. With every stop they made—

to the bank, to the blacksmith shop, and even to the preacher's home—it shrunk even more.

Tolliver had used his time in Bear Creek to plant seeds of doubt about Seb's character and that of the whole family. Even folks like the preacher, who talked about forgiveness on Sunday mornings, showed suspicion in their eyes and blamed Seb for Tolliver's presence in Bear Creek. When Seb mentioned what Tolliver had done to Matty, folks got scared. They didn't want to put themselves in danger.

And no one seemed to know where to find him.

As his hope shrank, his despair grew.

He'd gotten his family into this mess. And he knew Tolliver. The man wasn't going to stop until he'd had his revenge. Seb didn't know if Tolliver was a marksman. He didn't like the idea of any of them being outside for any length of time.

And Tolliver had already destroyed part of their livelihood by running those cattle off the cliff. It was a cruel thing to do. A sign of just how completely void Tolliver was of humanity.

How could Seb fight back without help? When he didn't know what Tolliver would do next?

It could be days or weeks before help arrived from Denver—if any was even coming.

SEB SAT at Matty's bedside. It was late, and dark had fallen outside the window.

It had been three days since he'd told his family the truth.

Matty's eyes were closed, his breathing low and even. In the past days, his brother had slipped in and out of consciousness.

Maxwell had said the head wound needed time to heal. He'd said that, after a few days, Matty should be able to stay conscious for longer periods.

It had been three days of tension.

The best plan that they had been able to come up with was to have all the women and children stay at the main house and the bunkhouse, which was the closest building.

The men slept in shifts. There were always at least two on watch.

They'd decided to bring the cattle out of the high field, and Penny and Rose—the two best horsewomen—had ridden along with them, which left more guns to be trained on the surrounding countryside as the cows moved slowly toward the homestead.

They didn't have enough resources—the summer had been dry and grass was sparse—to keep the cattle close for long. Seb could only pray that this situation would be resolved soon.

There'd been no sightings of Tolliver. Not even a boot print or a horse track. The sheriff had promised to keep watch for Tolliver in town, but he was a deputy short with Matty to help and Seb hadn't heard from the man since he and Jonas had gone for help. He prayed daily for Maxwell and Hattie to stay out of Tolliver's sights.

The lack of action was making everyone edgy.

And so was the fact that Seb had broken his family's trust. He'd been amazed and humbled that Pa and Ma harbored no judgment toward him. Even if Pa was disappointed to find out what a failure he was, he had hidden it well. It was the sideways glances that Seb had caught from Edgar and Davy that hurt.

His brothers had a right to be furious that he had brought this danger down on them and their families. He didn't know whether he could earn their trust back.

He desperately needed to talk to someone. But there wasn't time, not with the constant vigilance and watchfulness they were all experiencing. He'd come in here to give Catherine a break. Her two little ones were missing their mama, missing the familiarity of their normal routine.

He'd hoped his brother would have one of his lucid periods.

The door opened, and he glanced up to see Emma carefully maneuvering a tray through the door.

She must've known he was in here, because she whispered, "Is the bedside table empty?"

"Yes."

She moved to set the tray on it, doing so with only the slightest rattle. As if she'd done it many times.

Since the night he'd confessed, he hadn't been able to get more than a passing glance at her. She was always helping his ma or watching over the little ones. And not only were they both kept busy, but his brothers seemed to be conspiring to keep him away from her.

If Emma was in the kitchen serving lunch, one of his brothers would strike up a conversation that required Seb's participation until the opportunity had passed. She had been swinging Matty's oldest and Oscar's youngest beneath the big maple, careful to stay close to the house. He had been on his way from the barn to the house and only intended a small detour to say hello. But Oscar and Walt and Andrew had raced past him, engaging the little tykes and Emma in a game of tag. Seb had carried her laughter in his heart all afternoon.

And he hadn't missed the dark look from Oscar as his older brother had been passing by. Seb knew the interruption was on purpose.

He couldn't help but remember when Maxwell had been discouraged about wooing Hattie. All the brothers had ganged up on him and convinced him to make a fool of himself by reciting poetry to win her heart. When Edgar had been hung up on Fran, they'd formed a posse to confront him about his intentions.

It seemed that his brothers intended to interfere in his relationship with Emma, but not to help him. Nope. They were intent on keeping him away from her.

It hurt.

Right now it was all he could do to keep from going to her. Maybe he would've embraced her. But he forced himself to stay in the chair at Matty's bedside.

Meanwhile, the food on that tray was making his mouth water. The savory scent of venison and the yeasty scent of his ma's sweet rolls tickled his nose. There were sweet potatoes and something green. Maybe peas.

"That's a lot of food for an invalid."

She smiled a little. "Your mother sent it in for you. She said you missed supper because you were on patrol."

That was Ma, paying attention even though her house was overrun with children and daughters-in-law. Making sure every mouth got fed.

He shifted his feet in front of the chair. "I guess I'm not very hungry."

She picked up the plate and rounded the bend, delivering it to him.

He took it only because he knew she would wait him out. Stubborn woman.

"You need to keep your strength up. We don't know how long this will last."

He could only hope and pray Tolliver would make a move soon. Things couldn't go on this way. Tensions were high and tempers were short.

Matty remained still in the bed, eyes closed and unaware of their low voices.

For a moment, when Emma handed Seb the fork, he let his fingers close over hers.

She didn't pull away.

There was so much he wanted to say to her. But his brothers obviously thought she was better off without him.

And he was questioning everything. Maybe they were right.

He didn't know anymore.

The first bite of venison exploded on his tongue with flavor. He shoveled in another, practically inhaling the food.

He swallowed. "I guess I didn't realize how hungry I was."

"You should let your ma take care of you. She's missed out on doing it since you left."

A weak voice came from the bed. "She's right. Sometimes the women in our lives know better than we do."

Matty.

Seb set aside his plate and clasped his brother's hand as Emma went back around the bed to fetch Matty's bowl of broth.

"It's good to hear your voice," Seb said. If his voice was a little husky with emotion, he couldn't help it.

Matty turned his head slightly on the pillow, wincing. He must still be in pain. Guilt and shame sat on Seb's chest like a two-thousand-pound bull.

"Where's Catherine?"

"She needed some rest. She's been by your side this whole time." Emma's soft words seemed to reassure him.

Seb didn't know how much his brother was aware of. "We've got all the women and children staying close to the house. No one's going to get hurt."

Matty's eyes closed in a slow blink. "Good." He seemed to breathe easier at that.

Seb watched as Emma gently propped a pillow behind Matty's shoulders. She lifted a glass of water to his lips.

And then she helped settle the broth bowl so his brother could feed himself.

Seb couldn't keep his eyes off her, and she didn't have to turn her face for him to know that she was as aware of him as he was of her.

But his brother's sharp gaze—a lawman's gaze—didn't miss a thing.

"Seems like I missed something. Or you two have gotten closer since I've been out of it."

Seb felt the tips of his ears get hot.

It was Emma who answered, her voice soft but sure. "Nothing's settled yet."

"You can give me a hard time about that another day," Seb said. "Right now, if you feel up to it, I need you to try and remember what happened. How did Tolliver get the jump on you?"

Matty frowned. "A lot of it is still fuzzy. Irma Moses made a report that someone stole her prize hog."

The brothers shared a glance. Irma was still raising a hog each year for the founders' day exhibition? She must be at least eighty years old.

"She was sure someone had let him out. Her fence wasn't torn up or cut—I can't remember now why she thought someone was causing trouble." Matty pressed the heel of his hand to his temple as if thinking about it was making his head ache.

"I rode out to her place to take a look around. I was on my way back, skirting the Eldrich place because I didn't want to get caught in a conversation that would last all afternoon." The brothers shared a glance. Ma Eldrich could talk the ear off a mule.

Seb had forgotten this. Forgotten how he and his brothers could read each other without speaking. Forgotten what it felt like to be a part of the family and the community.

Matty's smile faded as he went on. "I met Richards—your Tolliver—at church once, I think. He seemed friendly. When he rode up to me and told me he'd seen what he thought was a body down in the creek, I believed him. We rode together until we reached a little gully. I went ahead of him, but he"—Matty shook his head—"he attacked me from behind. Got in a blow to my head that made me dizzy. I fought back. I'm pretty sure I got in at least one blow. I couldn't get to my rifle. That's all I remember."

It wasn't much to go on. Irma and the Eldriches lived south of Bear Creek. But that didn't mean Tolliver was staying nearby. He could've followed Matty out of town and attacked him.

They needed more clues. And Seb was out of ideas.

17

Cecilia jumped as the front door swung open. Her younger sister Velma darted inside, followed a few moments later by her adoptive mother, Sarah.

Cecilia quickly crumpled the paper in her hand and slipped it and the two other letters from the kitchen table into the pocket of her apron.

Velma scampered to her bedroom in the back of the house, but Sarah stopped in the kitchen. She smiled at Cecilia, but Cecilia couldn't help feeling that her mother's sharp eyes hadn't missed a thing.

It was difficult to be confined to such a small space. Cecilia understood the danger, but she chafed with little to no privacy.

"The bread has another hour to go," Cecilia said. "I was just getting ready to start the washing."

There was no missing the yeasty scent of rising bread.

And Cecilia had already lugged the washtub outside. She had two buckets for pumping water sitting on the step outside, waiting.

After the school term ended, she'd been welcomed back into the bosom of the family. Early on, Sarah had asked whether she would be returning the following year. Cecilia had been noncommittal.

Since then, Cecilia had sent several inquiries to nearby schools and to some of the instructors at the Cheyenne Normal School, where she'd received her teaching certificate.

Yesterday, Oscar, her adoptive father, and two of her uncles had gone to town, scouting for Tolliver. Oscar had brought back three letters addressed to her, giving them to her with raised brows, but she'd only slipped them into her pocket without comment.

This morning was the first time she'd been alone since. And though she'd only had a few moments to digest the news, it wasn't good.

The first two schools had no openings. The third had already filled their position for the next term.

Cecilia had sent out a dozen inquiries, and these were only three letters. But she couldn't help being disappointed.

One year as a teacher, and she was already a failure.

What was she going to do if she didn't get hired for the fall term?

She forced the thought away. She couldn't think like that. Surely someone would be willing to take a chance on her, even if she couldn't provide a reference from her last teaching job.

She couldn't countenance the thought of anything else. Her parents had paid for her schooling, and she was determined to pay them back. Oscar and Sarah had already done so much for her and her sisters when they'd taken them in when they'd been orphaned as young girls.

Cecilia knew what they had given up to bring three little girls into their marriage. The debt Cecilia owed them was one that might never be repaid. But Cecilia was determined to try.

"This morning your uncle found some tracks out west, past the creek," Sarah said. "Papa has asked us to stay close to the main house."

Cecilia nodded.

Sarah searched her face, and Cecilia couldn't help being a tiny bit grateful that Seb's arrival and the trouble he'd caused was taking the family's attention away from her.

She was deeply ashamed of what had happened during her spring term and how her job had ended. She was determined to make things right going forward.

She was never going to make a mistake again. When she got her next job, she would be above reproach. She would stay far away from all single men in the community. And the married ones to boot. She'd learned her lesson. Men couldn't be trusted.

All she had to do was find one school that would give her a chance.

Sarah's nose wrinkled, and she glanced out the window.

Cecilia followed her gaze, smelling smoke. What—?

Velma shrieked from the back bedroom at the same moment Cecilia caught sight of flames rising from the barn.

She rushed to the doorway, only a step behind Sarah.

In the distance, smoke billowed in a terrifying cloud.

SEB'S THROAT BURNED. His eyes watered. He couldn't draw a full breath, even with a wet handkerchief tied over his face.

It hadn't taken long to figure out that the fire had been set on purpose. There'd been no lightning strike to set it off. It had traversed the field in a wall of flames too wide to be accidental.

Every single person who could help was fighting the fire. Even Walt and Andrew were on the bucket brigade trying desperately to stop the flames, which were coming closer to the house every minute.

Oscar had wasted no time in hitching a pair of horses to the plow. He was attempting to turn over a wide enough swath of dirt to form a windbreak. It might be their only chance to save the family home.

One wall of the barn was burning, and they'd released all the horses from inside.

There was a storm brewing on the horizon, but right now the wind was against them, blowing ash and smoke into their eyes and making it impossible to draw a full breath. He prayed for the rain to hit fast and hard, to extinguish the fire.

Seb kept scouring the horizon. Wouldn't Tolliver want to watch? Was he out there right now?

Seb worked to beat down flames in the grass with a wet blanket. He felt a prickle of awareness as if the man's eyes were on him right now.

Seb was angry. Angry that someone would purposely burn down his family's livelihood. Angry that he had brought this down on them. It was his fault. All his fault.

Someone screamed.

He wheeled to see Velma's skirt had caught fire. Edgar was nearby and grabbed her, bodily pulling her away. He set her on the ground to smother the smoking fabric.

The wind gusted, blowing smoke into his face, and Seb lost sight of them for a moment.

He couldn't leave his post. Had to trust that his brother would protect Velma.

Tolliver had wanted to hurt his family. And he was doing it.

How could Seb fight against someone when he didn't know what direction the danger was coming from?

Jonas ran toward Seb, shouting and waving his arms. Seb backed away from the wall of flames.

"The barn's going to go. We need to get the women and kids to a safer spot."

Seb looked at his pa. Only Jonas's eyes were visible with the handkerchief over his face. They were filled with resignation.

Seb wanted to weep.

They were going to lose everything. And it was all Seb's fault.

"Pa, I'm sorry." He choked on the words, on the smoke.

Jonas clamped his shoulder, but that only made it worse. They jogged back toward the farmhouse. He wished he'd never come home.

And then Fran was running out of the house, terror in her expression. Rose was on her heels.

"We can't find Emma!"

EMMA LAY ON HER BELLY, halfway hanging off the horse of the man she'd known as Richards.

How could she have been so stupid?

She'd been inside, content that she was helping fight the fire by minding the children. But when Ida, who had been keeping up a running commentary from the window, had cried out that the barn was going up in flames, Emma had felt a fierce need to do something *more*.

She'd gone to stand on the back porch, hoping that someone would pass close enough for her to ask whether there was a way she could help.

And standing outside the house had been enough.

A strong arm had banded around her waist even as a hand clamped over her nose and mouth. She'd tried to struggle, but it'd been no use as Tolliver had dragged her around the side of the house—out of view of Seb and his family—and onto his horse.

Right now she felt like a sack of flour. A badly-used sack of flour.

The pommel horn dug into her side, but she dared not move, fearing she'd be thrown from the animal and break her neck.

Tears rolled down her face, but she'd stop screaming after the second blow to the side of her head. She could feel a knot forming above her ear.

She couldn't quite believe this was happening. The smell of smoke had lessened and finally faded altogether, which meant they had already covered a significant distance.

She had no sense of direction, only air rushing past as the man pushed the horse in a wild gallop. How long had it been? They could already be miles away.

Seb must be crazy with worry. And Fran.

If Emma could just find a way to escape... But that was an unrealistic hope, wasn't it?

She didn't know where she was.

Without her sight, she didn't know if there were any houses nearby. Any people working in the fields who might be willing to help her. She didn't even know if there was a copse of trees or a gully that she could escape into and avoid detection.

She tried to remember the different ways Seb and Edgar had taught her to defend herself, back when she'd been on the run from Underhill. But her mind was flying in so many directions, like a flock of sparrows scattering at the sound of a gunshot.

Panic was doing her no good. She couldn't jump from the horse. She didn't know where they were going or how to figure it out.

Her hands ached where they had been bound in front of her. She focused on that pain. Focused on changing it.

If she could free her wrists... She didn't know what she would do when they stopped. She knew that his horse couldn't keep up this pace for long. Not with two passengers. Wherever Tolliver was taking her, it must be close.

She wouldn't have much time. But if she could loosen the rope around her wrists, maybe she could somehow engineer an escape.

18

T he barn was lost.

Even as he raced toward Bear Creek, Seb couldn't get the image of fire crawling up the wall and toward the roof out of his head. He would never forget that one last look as he and Davy and Edgar rode toward town.

Only minutes after they'd gone, the first fat raindrops had begun to fall. Maybe the house would be saved yet.

He didn't know if riding to town was the right choice, but he couldn't go after Tolliver alone. Not if he had a chance of bringing back Emma alive.

He could only hope that they would find help. Even if everyone in town had been poisoned against him, surely some would ride out when they learned that Emma was in danger. Emma had never harmed anyone. She was pure and sweet, everything that he wasn't.

He rode through town like a crazy person, causing a

pair of horses harnessed to a wagon outside the mercantile to rear in their traces. He didn't care. Someone called out to him. He didn't hear.

He pulled up outside the sheriff's office, swung himself out of the saddle, and ran up the steps.

He burst through the door, surprising the sheriff and a tall man standing near his desk.

"Sheriff, I need your help." He realized who was standing there. "Levi. You're here."

The last time he'd seen the US Marshal had been back in Colorado. After Daniel had introduced them, Levi had immediately whisked him away to the safe house.

The sheriff's expression was clear of the suspicion he'd showed last week when Jonas and Seb had visited him.

"I got your telegraph, son. Heard you were having some trouble."

Seb felt tears rise to his eyes, but he didn't feel any humiliation. Emma was the only thing that mattered now. "Tolliver set fire to my pa's land. The barn was going up in flames when I left."

The sheriff came halfway around his desk. "We can start rounding up some folks to help."

Seb shook his head. "It's worse. Emma Morris is missing. She's blind. She wouldn't have wandered off, not with the fire raging. Tolliver took her."

The Marshal looked grave. He knew what Tolliver was capable of. "You got any idea where he took her to?"

Seb shook his head. "I didn't have time to search for

tracks, not with my family fighting the fire. I need help." And now, the rain would likely wash any tracks away.

He swallowed hard. He'd been too afraid to ask for help in Denver. Too ashamed and sure that he could get himself out of the mess he'd made for himself. But he needed help now. "I've got to find her. Please, can you help?"

Emma was terrified.

But at least she was off that horse.

Tolliver had roughly thrown her from the horse. She'd landed badly on her bound wrists, still tied in front of her. They hurt, but she could move them, could use them if she could get them free. He'd then dragged her inside what she'd determined might be an old shack. Once she'd heard the door latch and his footsteps fade, she'd stood on shaky legs and paced the perimeter with her hands outstretched in front of her. The space was tiny. Smaller than her bedroom. It smelled of mildew and animals. Her feet splashed in shallow puddles and rain dripped on her head.

Tolliver hadn't spoken one word to her, just left. She tried the door for good measure, but it was latched from outside.

She was soaked through, cold and miserable.

By the time they'd arrived, she'd almost had her wrists free. Now, she worked the ropes again. Her wrists protested with each movement, but she kept at it until the ropes loosened and fell away. Blood rushed to her abused hands, tingling and stinging as she flexed them.

He hadn't checked the ropes when he'd thrown her in this small room. Did he think her helpless because of her blindness? Maybe.

What was he planning to do with her? Would he come back soon?

She didn't have her walking stick, but she used her feet to test the floor before each step. She made her way to the door, and while she recoiled from the feel of spiderwebs and dust, she forced herself to feel around its edge. Was there a way to unlatch it from inside?

No.

But the land beneath the shack had shifted, and there was a sizable crack between the door and its frame. If she could find something thin and long, she could perhaps raise the bar on the outside that blocked her exit.

Even if she could get out, she had no idea where she was. What if she was in the middle of an open field? What if he was out there watching her?

She knew Seb would try to find her. Edgar too. She wanted to be alive when they did. And to help them out, if at all possible.

Was there a way she could help them find her? If she could build a fire, smoke could be seen for miles around. But if Tolliver hadn't left the property, he'd come back and hurt her worse than the few blows he'd already landed. She didn't even know if she could find anything to help her start a fire. And she didn't want to suffocate herself if she couldn't get out.

As she'd methodically worked her way around the shack minutes ago, she'd tripped on two empty wash buckets and stumbled over a pile of oddly-shaped wood and metal in one corner.

Was there any chance there would be something useful?

She was tentative and careful as she sorted through the pile. She wasn't worried about splinters, but a sharp edge could cut her hand.

She found a metal pick that she tucked into the pocket of her skirt. Maybe it would do to jimmy the bar on the door open.

There were no lucky finds like flint and tinder.

She did discover a part of what might've been a rake or shovel handle that she could use as a walking stick.

At the bottom of the pile was a worn and holey piece of canvas.

She wrapped it around her shoulders, hoping to stay a little dry.

Thunder cracked, and the sound of rain on the roof grew louder, more constant.

She was losing hope.

In this deluge, whatever tracks Tolliver's horse made would be erased. Seb would have no idea where to look for her. And visibility would be terrible if he did catch sight of this old shack.

She could only hope that the rain stopped the fire at the Whites' property.

If Seb wouldn't be able to find her, it would be up to her to escape.

It took her several tries with the pick to jimmy the latch and get the door open. Her hands were slick with sweat, her fingers shaking from the cold. Once the latch was out of the way, she only let the door open a crack. Only far enough that the latch wouldn't fall back into place and trap her again.

She sat for a moment with her back against the wall, listening to the rain and trying to pray.

Where was Tolliver? Was he out in the rain? Or was there a house or another structure—a barn?—nearby? Should she make a run for it?

Her brain wanted to kick her back to the times she'd been stuck in bed after her blindness.

That hopelessness, the realization that everything had changed and there was nothing she could do to fix it.

Back then, Daniel had saved her. He'd convinced her she still had a life worth living.

But there was no Daniel here. No Seb. No one but herself.

She was the one who'd gotten out of the bed at her brother's urging.

She'd had to find the strength to figure out how to take care of herself, to learn to cook without being able to see what she was doing, to make a new life for herself, new friends for herself, in Denver.

She could fight her way out of here.

She strained her ears to listen. Was Tolliver close?

All she could hear was the rain and occasional claps of thunder.

When she could bear it no longer, she opened the door and slipped through.

She didn't know what the landscape around the shack looked like. But she decided that, since the door was on this side of the shack, she wanted to be on the other side.

With her walking stick, she carefully felt her way around the building, quickly ducked past the corner. She ran into a fence. Three rails, like a... corral!

A soft whicker from nearby had her slipping through the fence. Approaching a strange horse was a risk. She didn't know the animal, and she couldn't see it.

But she had to go. She might only have one chance to escape.

She felt a presence nearby and froze. She remained perfectly still. Extended one arm, hand outstretched.

There was a huff. And then a soft nose brushed into her palm.

19

The torrential rains had washed away any tracks Tolliver might've left.

Seb was desperate to take action.

It killed him to think about Emma, alone in Tolliver's clutches. Was she all right? Was she frightened? Hurt?

The only bright side about delaying was that the sheriff had managed to round up a posse of ten while Marshal Levi and Seb's brothers had done more questioning in town.

Sam Castlerock—the banker and Penny's brother—had recalled Tolliver riding north out of town several times.

It was the barest of hints. Tolliver could be anywhere. Holed up in a cave. Living in a long-abandoned dugout, camouflaged on the prairie. Even holed up in the woods somewhere. But it was a place to start.

They couldn't delay anymore. They were wasting time that Emma might not have.

"Our best guess is north," Marshal Levi said.

His words jarred something loose in Seb's brain.

Cora Beth's homestead was north of town. She'd seen a stranger around. And her instincts had told her that whoever was watching her place was dangerous.

What if it had been Tolliver?

When Seb had helped her get to the train station, he hadn't had an inkling of what was coming. He hadn't thought to ask her for a description of the man who was stalking her.

Was it a coincidence? Or divine providence?

Seb quickly explained his theory to Levi and the sheriff. It was as good a guess as they could make. With the posse following, they rode out toward Cora Beth's house as fast as they could push their horses.

Her place was a pretty meadow in a valley. The higher vantage point made it easy to see the house from far away. The rain had stopped. They were a quarter-mile from the homestead when Seb caught sight of the empty corral.

His heart plummeted.

If Tolliver was there, he would need a place to keep his horse. And there was no horse in sight.

He'd been sustained by wild hope, thinking that, after all these hours, they'd find Tolliver and Emma. But now, that hope had proved futile. Tolliver could've taken her anywhere.

He was ready to ride on—he didn't know where to—

but the sheriff wanted to knock on the door of the empty house just to be sure.

Seb was wheeling his horse, intending to urge his brothers to join him in continuing the search, when the first shot rang out from inside the house.

He reined in, his eyes scanning to see what had happened.

The sheriff had dismounted not far from the house. He was still standing but had been spun around, blood spurting from a spot in his shoulder that bloomed red. His horse spooked and bolted. The man staggered toward the house. Another shot rang out and hit the ground a few feet beyond the sheriff. Lucky miss.

The posse and Seb's brothers scattered, spurring their horses to get out of the line of fire.

Another shot rang out but didn't hit anyone.

Seb glanced back to check on the sheriff, who now stood with his back pressed against the house, one hand on the wound at his shoulder. He was still on his feet, though blood stained his shirt and dripped down his arm.

It had to be Tolliver. If he was alone in the house, they could surround him. He couldn't take them all out, no matter if he had dozens of bullets.

"Emma!" Seb shouted. "Emma?"

There was no answer.

Tolliver was no sharpshooter. He kept missing. As long as he kept moving, Seb was reasonably sure he wouldn't be hit.

Where was Tolliver's horse? Where was Emma? Was

she inside? Seb nudged his horse into a run and headed for the ramshackle shack near the corral. Edgar followed, pulling a pistol from his hip.

From the front of the house, the sheriff's voice called out, "If you walk out now with your hands up, we won't shoot."

A shot fired. Another.

Guess Tolliver didn't want to surrender.

Both Seb and Edgar rode up to the shack, dismounting before the horses stopped, and when Edgar slapped his mount's rump, Seb did the same. Better that the animals were out of range if Tolliver started shooting in their direction.

"Emma?" Seb called out.

There was no answer. The door was ajar. When Seb opened it, he saw the small room was empty.

There were muddy tracks on the floor. A jumble of tools and pieces of wood were scattered in the back corner.

It was shadowed, but there was enough light for him to see that there was something scratched in the floor in the dirt. It was messy, like a child had scrawled the word. It was smudged slightly from raindrops that must've leaked through the roof.

He got closer, crouched down, and touched the scrawl.

It was his name.

Emma had been there.

He exited the building to find that his brother had crossed the yard and sidled up to the back window of the house. He had his rifle trained on something inside.

Another shout came from the front of the house.

Tolliver had been warned to come out. He hadn't.

"Take the shot," Seb called softly to his brother.

Edgar let loose a bullet from his rifle. Glass shattered. The recoil knocked him back from the window.

Edgar shouted, "I don't know if he's down for good."

Other men—Seb's brothers and the posse-had come close and now swarmed the door. There were shouts from inside, and then silence.

Seb darted across the yard to the house. He burst through the back door.

Tolliver lay on the floor, gutshot.

He wasn't going to survive that. Seb felt the tiniest twinge of guilt for the relief that flowed. But where was Emma?

Levi shook his head.

"She isn't here," Edgar said.

"She was," Seb said. "She wrote my name." He moved to stand over Tolliver. "Where is she?"

The man only stared at him, silent.

"Where is she?" Seb leaned down to look into his eyes. "Tell me."

"He's not going to tell you," Levi said. "He knows it'll hurt you worse for him to stay silent."

Tolliver coughed, and blood flecked his lips. His breathing was shallow and rattled in his chest.

Seb desperately glanced around at the faces of the men who stood inside.

"There was no horse in the corral," he said. "What if Emma escaped and took off?"

Edgar shrugged.

The sheriff looked skeptical. "She's blind."

"Doesn't mean she's not resourceful." Emma could've done it.

"But where would she go?" Levi asked. His expression was grave.

It was nearly dark, and with the rain that had fallen, it could be dangerous.

Seb felt a helpless panic overtaking him. "I don't know."

He'd ridden to her rescue, but was he too late?

EMMA HAD GOTTEN herself into trouble for sure.

Based on the sounds of crickets chirping and the occasional call of a whip-poor-will, night had fallen. The only other sound was the horse's footsteps as they plodded along.

The animal had been both bridled and saddled when Emma'd found him. She'd seen it as an answer to her prayers. She couldn't have ridden bareback. The stirrups had been too long, but that didn't matter.

She'd escaped.

She didn't know whether Tolliver was following her. She didn't know whether he had another horse or if he would be on foot. All she knew was the further away she got, the better off she was. If she could by some chance stumble on a neighbor's house, she would be safe.

She was managing at a slow pace until the horse balked. She knew that if she dismounted, she wouldn't be able to get back on. She'd used the corral's fence to mount the first time. Out here, she'd be stuck.

She didn't have any way of knowing what was in front of her. Should she try and turn to head another direction? That seemed dangerous too. What if she ended up heading back the way she'd come?

She urged the horse forward, praying that she wasn't heading into something dangerous. She felt the horse's body move. Tilt forward. She almost lost her balance. They must've reached a ravine or a steep hillside

She held onto the pommel, but each slow downward step jarred her.

And then the horse lurched, and the movement was so unexpected that she lost her balance completely. Unable to right herself, she tumbled to the side. She tried to grab onto the saddle, but the animal was slick from the rain.

She landed hard on her shoulder, losing her breath in the fall.

She heard the horse take several steps away as she tried to catch her breath.

Her fingers dug into the muddy hillside, not as steep as what she feared but still terrifying to navigate. Her walking stick had fallen away, and she scrambled on the ground, trying to locate it.

It was no use.

Her hands were scratched from the rocks and tough vegetation. She couldn't find her stick, and if she stood up and walked, she might stumble on this rocky hillside. She couldn't reach the horse.

The same desperation and hopelessness that she'd fought off earlier threatened to overwhelm her again.

What had she been thinking, coming out here like this? She'd been afraid of Tolliver. But now she was lost in a ravine in the dark with no help coming and no way to escape.

Tears fell down her cheeks. She wasn't going to give up. Just like she wasn't going to let Seb give up on their relationship.

She stayed low to the ground, crawling up the hill on her hands and knees. She scratched her face when she ran into a thorny bush. She wept in her fright, but she didn't stop climbing.

And then she heard a far-off shout. She strained her ears again for the sound. And prayed she wasn't dreaming it.

"Emma!"

Someone was out there. Someone was shouting her name.

Was it Tolliver? He knew her name. He'd sat across from her only a few days ago, pretending to be a friend. She resolved not to answer. She didn't know what she was going to do if he was following her.

And then another shout filled her heart with hope.

That was Seb.

"Help!" The word tore from her throat.

The other voice stopped.

Her heart beat painfully in her chest.

"Emma!"

"I'm here! Help!"

Moments that seemed like hours later, she heard footsteps somewhere above her. "Emma?"

"Seb!" she called out. "I'm down here."

She heard the scraping first and then felt tiny rocks cascading down the hill. They rattled against her clothing.

"Emma." Seb's voice, just a few feet above her now. "Thank God."

A soft sob escaped. He was really here.

She felt the disturbance in the air as he neared before she felt his presence. She reached for him, and he met her. He clasped her upper arms, pulling her into him, holding her close.

"Are you hurt? Did he hurt you?"

"I'm all right."

And she was because he was here. He'd come for her.

He was shaking, or maybe she was. He leaned back slightly, his hands coming to cup her jar, slide into her hair. She winced when his fingers touched the tender spot where Tolliver had struck her.

"I'm sorry." He must've seen her flinch. "What—?"

"It's a little tender. Nothing's broken."

He brushed a tender kiss across her lips, then held her close again.

"What about you?" she asked.

"I'm fine. We cornered Tolliver at Cora Beth's place. The sheriff got hit, but nobody else got hurt. I've got a posse and half my brothers up at the top of the ravine waiting to get a look at you."

She clung to him, so thankful he'd found her.

"I'm sorry," he whispered into her hair. "Sorry it took so long to get to you."

"Maybe I should've stayed," she said.

"I saw your message in that shack. You were thinking ahead. You got out of there."

"I knew you'd come. I just didn't know when, or what he'd—"

He stopped her babbling words with a kiss.

This time they were interrupted by a shout from above. "Is she all right?"

He gave a little laugh as he broke the kiss.

She buried her face in his chest. "Your brothers."

He sighed, a gust of breath against her forehead. "We've got a mostly dry saddle blanket up there. Let's get you warmed up. And let's go home."

Nothing had ever sounded better to her. "What about the homestead? The fire?"

"The barn is gone. We left in a rush but I'd guess the rain kept the fire from claiming the house."

Tears flowed in relief.

She let him guide her to the top of the ravine, only slipping once. He quickly caught her with his hand beneath her elbow and another at her waist.

It was only a few moments until they reached flat ground, and Edgar swept her into a hug. "Your sister is worried sick about you."

"I'm all right."

Seb was right there when Edgar let her go. "She's cold and wet. We need to get her warm."

He wrapped a blanket around her, and when Edgar would've protested, Seb silenced him with a no-nonsense growl.

In moments, she was sitting atop Seb's horse with him, his arm snug around her waist. She let her head rest on his shoulder, the blanket providing warmth, but his arm and his steadiness behind her providing even more.

She nodded off, overwhelmed by her ordeal and the knowledge that she was finally going home.

20

I t had been almost dawn by the time the procession rode up to the family homestead.

After the terrifying experience, Emma slept until noon the next day. The afternoon was spent helping everyone settle back into their own homes while the men took stock of the damage to the land and the burnt barn and trying to find temporary places to stable the horses that had been displaced by the fire.

Maxwell and Hattie had spent hours trying to save Tolliver's life. Maxwell had been able to remove the bullet from his gut some hours into the surgery, but Tolliver had taken too much trauma and had passed away on the operating table. The US Marshal had been there as a witness. He'd already headed back to his home base in Colorado.

The next day was Sunday, and the family had decided to worship together on the homestead instead of going into town. After a time of singing and prayer together at the picnic tables, the children begin to get restless.

When the adults dismissed them to play for a while before lunch, they ran off with shrieks of joy and delight. The danger had passed, and as far as the children were concerned, everything was going to be all right.

It was the adults who realized the gravity of the situation.

"I've got something I'd like to say." Seb's voice rang out in the quiet moment.

Emma had been relieved when he'd come to sit by her this morning. She'd barely been around him the day before, only when he'd stopped by for a short walk as Fran was tucking her little ones into bed. He'd been subdued and quiet. And Emma hadn't pushed. Seb had to have been almost as terrified as she with all the events of the day before.

She thought they had time to get things settled between them. But this morning he'd been silent beside her, as still as the mighty maple that stood out in front of Jonas and Penny's house. She'd almost gotten up the courage to take his hand in hers. But a sudden sense of foreboding had held her still.

Now, he turned his body slightly and addressed his family from where he sat beside her.

"I'm sorry for bringing this calamity down on all of you. I thought I'd escaped from that part of my life. It was my bad choices that brought Tolliver here." She heard him swallow. "I nearly got Emma killed. The barn's gone. And so is the hay we needed for this winter."

Penny spoke up from somewhere to Emma's right. "That wasn't your fault, honey."

She felt the shudder go through him. "Tolliver only came here because of me."

It was a surprise when the normally soft-spoken Maxwell was next to speak. "We needed a little more adventure in our lives. Things were getting boring without you."

"Maybe not this much adventure," Matty added. He was up and out of bed for the first time.

It might've been Catherine who gave a teary laugh at that.

She could still feel the tension emanating from Seb beside her.

The Emma who had escaped from Tolliver's clutches yesterday was still inside of her. She didn't have to wait for him to announce his intentions. She reached out and touched his knee. Her fingers bumped into the back of his hand, just like she'd hoped. She slid her fingers around and clasped it. Awareness prickled as if someone were watching her. Maybe lots of someones. She didn't care.

But Seb didn't hold her hand. He stayed perfectly still, his hand stiff and flat on his knee.

"The folks in town were right about me. I'm not the same man I was when I left. Because of that, I brought a heap of trouble down on us."

Oh, Seb. He was being crushed by the guilt he was trying to carry alone.

"Are you planning on boxing anytime soon?" That from Oscar.

"Of course not, " Seb snapped.

"Starting your own criminal enterprise?" That was from Matty, a teasing tone in his voice.

Seb scoffed. "I just want to come home. Be a part of this family again."

"Seems like you've got some intentions of settling down to start your own family," Davy called out.

Someone whistled.

Seb's hand twitched beneath hers.

Someone shushed Davy, but Edgar's growl made it to Emma's ears. "He better have the right intentions in mind."

Emma's face went hot, but she didn't let go of Seb.

"I'll make my intentions known to Emma first if you don't mind, you ornery lot." He flipped his hand and threaded his fingers with hers, and the anxious butterflies bettering the inside of her stomach finally settled. "There's a lot that needs to be set right on the homestead before I can think about settling down. After all the trouble I've caused, maybe I should leave for a while. Find work and send money home—"

There was a chorus of "nos" from all around.

"You just got back," Oscar said.

"You can't leave now," Matty echoed.

"What happened to the barn and the crops is a family matter," said Jonas. "It's not for you to fix alone."

Some tension left Seb. "After the drought last year, can we afford to rebuild?" he asked.

The silence was fraught with unspoken worries.

"Things were going to be tight this year anyway," Jonas said finally. "We may be able to get Sam to loan us the money to rebuild the barn."

"But the crops..." Oscar started.

The loss was bad.

But the hope in Emma's heart gave her the courage to speak out. "I'd like to contribute."

The murmurs all around suddenly silenced.

Her heart soared in her chest. "Ever since your family took me in, I've felt this place was my home. I have plenty of money just sitting in the bank. I'd like to give it to you. To rebuild."

"Where'd you get it from?" Matty asked, the teasing tone still in his voice.

"She's an author, silly." Susie, chiming in.

"How did you know?" Emma asked.

"Because she's a nosy busybody." Cecilia's criticism seemed to roll right off of the younger woman.

"I saw a book on your nightstand and borrowed it. E.J. Morris isn't that original of a name to use, you know. It wasn't hard to figure out, especially when I read about your character switching a dress for breeches when she was on the run."

Emma's blush blazed hot in her face. Beside her, Seb had gone silent. She could feel the weight of his gaze on her.

It was Fran who asked, "You wrote about that?"

Emma was proud of her work. "Just used that part. I didn't write about what happened to us."

"I figure some of us handsome and tough-as-nails-cowboys inspired your stories," Oscar called. There was a round of chuckles.

But none from Seb, who still sat silently beside her.

When the chuckles had died down, it was he who spoke. "Emma, that's your money. You earned it. And this is a family matter."

"Then I guess you better hurry up and make me a part of the family," she said.

There is a soft hoot from one of the brothers, but Seb let go of her hand.

A buzzing in her ears followed the loss of the contact. She felt bereft without him by her side.

As the silence grew around them awkwardly, she couldn't help but wonder if she'd made a huge blunder.

SEB'S breath was coming too fast. His heartbeat thrummed in his ears. He couldn't do this here, in front of his family, their eyes watching him so expectantly.

He stood. "Emma, take a walk with me?"

Fran looked as if she wanted to say something to him, or maybe take a piece out of his hide, but Edgar put a hand on her forearm, and she remained in her seat.

Emma stood slowly, as full of grace as always.

He led the way past the house toward the maple tree,

where his brothers wouldn't be able to hear every single thing he said.

Every time he looked at her, he remembered how close he'd come to losing her.

Her steps faltered. "Are you angry? Or... did I embarrass you?"

A few more steps, they reached the sheltering branches, and he stopped and turned to face her, though he limited himself to taking her hands in his. He needed all his wits about him for this conversation.

"Why would I be embarrassed that the most beautiful, most courageous, most intelligent woman I know claims she wants to marry me?"

Some of the tension she carried in her shoulders released. The fine lines at the corner of her mouth relaxed.

"When we... first declared ourselves," she said, "I would never have been so forward."

Surely she'd been around his brothers enough to know that what she'd said wasn't out of line.

He squeezed her hands gently. "I like knowing where I stand with you." He let go of one of her hands and raised his to rub over his mouth.

"What's the matter?" she asked.

He huffed a little half-laugh, though it didn't ring with mirth. "I came home with these grand plans. I was going to make things right with my family. And look at what trouble I caused for them. I was going to come and find you, to promise that I'd changed. Tell you how much I loved you and convince you to give me a chance. And here you are, waiting for me. Ready to save my family with your generosity."

He didn't know how he could accept it. The money she was willing to part with for the sake of his family was a big deal. Maybe his Pa would want to find a way to pay her back someday. But it was the gift of Emma herself that Seb didn't see how he could ever deserve.

Her eyes were luminous. "You love me?" she asked in a small voice.

Her uncertainty, even after she'd declared herself in front of his whole family, was too much. He crushed her to his chest, bending his head close to press his cheek against hers. "How could I not? You are... everything. And I'll spend the rest of my life trying to be the man you deserve. If you'll have me."

It wasn't much of a proposal. He cleared his throat and made himself inch back from her, taking both of her hands in his again. "Emma, will you marry me?"

"I think you already have your answer. Yes." Her lips trembled, and as he bent toward her, thinking to claim a kiss. But she tucked her chin to her chest. "I love you, too. And you don't have to do anything to earn it. It's a gift."

Emotion swamped his chest, expanding like a loaf of bread dough he'd once watched his ma bake. Spreading to fill all the cracks in his heart that had been damaged when he'd walked away from his family.

He cupped her cheek, swept his thumb across her soft skin. She was a gift. And he aimed to show her how much he cherished her every day that the Lord gave them together. He tipped her chin up and lowered to meet her. She responded to his kiss sweetly.

From far away, he heard one of his brothers holler, "I think she said yes."

A series of hoots and hollers rose, and Emma broke from his kiss with a smile.

"You knew what you were getting into," he reminded her.

"I did."

And it was a miracle she didn't seem to mind his rowdy brothers. He said, "We're both home now, and your family will be giving us a hard time for a while."

Home.

He put his arm around her shoulder as they walked back to her sister and his family—their family. It hadn't been that long ago that he'd thought this would never happen. A homecoming with Ma and Pa, his past behind him.

A new life his for the taking.

All the bad was behind him.

He was ready.

EPILOGUE

"Why are you reading the end first?"

"I want to see if the cowboy wins her heart."

"Is there any kissing?"

"Hey, why is the bad guy named Edgar?"

"Wonder if my name made it in there."

Emma sat in the corner of the family room in Jonas and Penny's home and listened to the rustle of turning pages as Seb's brothers read her brand new dime novel.

Autumn had arrived and with it bitter morning temperatures. The fire had been laid this morning, but now it was only coals, giving off only hints of the warmth it had provided earlier.

She clutched a cup of coffee between her hands and found herself smiling as the brothers teased about her latest book. A trunk full of her author's copies had arrived on the train yesterday, and Oscar had brought them back when he'd gone to town.

Ever since Seb's brothers had discovered she was a published author, they'd been taking turns reading the only copy of her first book that she'd brought with her to the homestead.

She could've asked Daniel to send along the trunk of copies that had remained at his Denver home when she had returned to Wyoming, but Seb had hinted that it would be more fun to let his brothers fight over a single copy. And she had to admit that he had been right.

Now, their teasing filled the room. And this moment was exactly what she'd been dreaming about ever since Fran had married Edgar all those years ago.

She and Seb had been married for three months, and she was happier than she'd ever been. She'd been accepted into the family and given the same teasing treatment that all of the other sisters-in-law received.

She loved every second.

She and Seb were already talking about a plan to prank Ricky when he and his family arrived for Christmas. Which reminded her that she needed to put a book in the mail for him.

"Did they get to the part where I rescue the cowgirl yet?" Seb's voice came from close behind her. He must've leaned against the back of the sofa for his murmur to be so close to her ear. His breath tickled her neck, and he snuck a kiss against her jaw.

Of course someone saw.

"Seb kissed Emma!" That was Walt's voice.

Thankfully, his older brothers were too absorbed in the book to pay the younger any mind.

"I told you I don't write about real people," she reminded her husband in a fierce whisper.

"That's right. If you wrote about me, it would be so unbelievably heroic that no one would believe any of it."

One of Seb's brothers—she thought it was Matty—groaned. "You're mighty full of yourself," he called out.

"Not as much as you are," Seb called back.

He was happy to joke with his brothers, but Emma knew that he still had some deep wounds from his past.

They'd talked at length in their snug little cabin, mostly during the quiet part of the night, huddled together under the quilt in their bed. Even though it didn't make sense, he admitted that he often worried she'd leave him. She knew it was because of the way he'd been orphaned at such a young age.

She'd taken to reciting the same vows she'd promised on their wedding day. *For richer or for poorer, in sickness and in health, till death do we part.* It seemed to help settle him.

Now, she held her coffee in her lap with one hand while she reached up with the other.

He caught her hand gently, the calluses on his palm reminding her of all the work he was putting in to help my family homestead.

It turned out the family hadn't needed all of the funds in her bank account. Enough had remained to buy lumber for a small cabin. They'd built near Fran and Edgar.

And she'd just sold another book, the one that she'd finish dictating to Phillip just as Seb had reappeared in her life.

Her new husband had teased her that he wasn't sure whether he could approve of her working so closely with Philip for hours on end. He had joked that maybe he would learn how to type and buy a typewriter. She'd reassured him with kisses that he had nothing to be jealous about. She'd never felt romantic inclinations toward Phillip. Seb believed her, even if he joked about it.

But she was already arranging to dictate her next dime novel with someone from the ranch at her side. Maybe Ida could do her schoolwork nearby.

"Want to sneak away?" her husband asked.

His nearness caused a delicious shiver down her spine, and she allowed him to help her out of her seat and around the jumble of legs and skirts as everyone continued reading in the family room.

No doubt there would be more teasing later, but she didn't mind.

She followed Seb out of the house and into the noon sunshine.

OUTSIDE, Seb led Emma to the corral, where he had two horses saddled and tied off, waiting for them. They'd already slipped into their coats.

"We're going riding?" Her voice lilted with surprise and happiness.

He couldn't help stealing a kiss, gratified when her hands came up to link behind his neck as she kissed him back.

He would spend the rest of his life making her happy if it was up to him.

One of the horses whickered, and he broke off the kiss, squeezing her waist and then letting her go.

Shortly after her flight from Tolliver, when she'd ridden blind across the countryside she didn't know, she'd mentioned that she wanted to learn to ride.

Since then, he'd spent a little time every day training a sweet bay mare that Oscar had known would be perfect for the job. No matter how far Seb rode, when he turned her loose on her own the mare always returned to the barn. He rewarded her with grain and extra apples each time to reinforce the importance of coming home. The horse was smart and strong and familiar with the land.

He knew Emma was just about ready to go on her first solo ride. But not today.

Now was the perfect time to escape. His brothers were distracted by the new book, it was a lazy autumn afternoon, and the chores were done. He had Emma all to himself, and he didn't intend to squander this time.

Emma used her walking stick, a usual fixture in her hand, to navigate to the corral.

"She's saddled and ready to go," he said. "About three steps in front of you."

Emma moved forward, trusting his estimation of the

distance. She extended her hand and gently brushed the horse's neck with her fingers.

"Give me a boost?" she asked.

He made a little pocket out of his hands, and she used it as a step to boost herself into the saddle.

She smoothed out her skirts and tucked her feet into the stirrups, and he handed her the reins. She barely waited for him to mount up himself before she was guiding the horse across the yard toward the open meadow behind the big house.

He loved it that her confidence had grown in the few short weeks they'd been practicing together.

They rode across the land his family had spent almost two decades taming. Crisp autumn wind made Emma's cheeks pink and rusted the colorful leaves on the aspens. They rode past the ridge that was a sort of a boundary line that separated the mountain meadow from the lower areas where cattle grazed.

At one point, a rabbit hopped out of the tall grass, likely startled by their horses. While Seb had to rein in his gelding, he was thrilled to see that Emma's horse only gave a snort at the interruption and kept walking.

For her part, Emma was relaxed and in control in the saddle.

When they arrived at the mountain pond, the water was still as a mirror, reflecting the sky and mountains.

He and Emma dismounted, and he started unpacking the picnic from his saddlebag while she ground tied the horses nearby. He laid out the bounty that he'd sweet-talked Ma into packing up for him.

"You outdid yourself," she said when she joined him on the blanket and he pressed a plate into her hand. "What's all this for?"

"I thought we could celebrate your new book."

Her lips twitched in a smile. "I thought that was what they were doing back at the house."

He gave a disgruntled sniff. "Those hooligans don't know how to appreciate fine literature."

She giggled, and he couldn't help chuckling along with her.

He was glad she loved being with his family. It took a special kind of woman to put up with the teasing his brothers could dish out. The fact that Emma wanted to pull her own kind of pranks was just a bonus.

"Does there have to be a reason for me to sneak away and steal some time with my wife?"

"I guess not."

He would never forget the warm, secretive smile that she gave him. Or the way his chest still puffed out with pride when he said the word *wife*.

Sometimes he had trouble believing it was true. Having Emma at his side had to be the biggest blessing anybody could ever receive.

They finished their meal and lay down on the blanket on their backs with their heads together. He picked out patterns in the swirling clouds against the blue sky while she told him what secrets the wind whispered to her.

They dreamed together about what they might be doing in a year or three years.

He was still pressing his case, trying to talk her into writing a book about the time when Fran had snuck along on a cattle drive.

She could fictionalize some of what had happened, but he had a feeling her readers would love a story like that.

A few hours later, just before they mounted up, Emma took his hand and leaned close, laying her head on his shoulder. "I love you, Seb."

He brushed a kiss on her forehead. "I'm never going to tire of hearing you say that. I love you, too."

Their quiet, peaceful time had to come to an end. They headed back to the big house and the chaos that awaited with his ornery pack of brothers and her sister and nieces and nephews galore.

And he couldn't be happier about it.

He'd taken a long and twisting road to get here. He'd found himself in the valley, and God had pulled him back out of the darkness. Now, he was living on the mountaintop. He could see so much light and so much brightness all around him. All the time.

He would never take it for granted. He was blessed indeed.

EPILOGUE 2

Cecilia stepped out of the buggy with shaking legs. She nodded to Oscar, who'd driven her this far, and he clucked to the horse and moved away from the tiny schoolhouse and toward the boardinghouse down the street with a sign that proclaimed they served breakfast.

Things had settled down back home since Tolliver had been captured and killed. Emma and Seb were married. Susie was flirting with any man in pants, as usual.

The school term was set to begin in one week. This position seemed to be her last chance.

She smoothed down the heavy traveling skirt she wore to no avail. Wrinkles from riding in the buggy since before dawn weren't going away. It was now well after lunchtime, and her stomach reminded her that she hadn't eaten the lunch Sarah had packed for her.

Her nerves had her tied up in knots, her stomach too wobbly to eat.

She needed this job. She hated the thought of disappointing Sarah and Oscar. But more than that, of disappointing herself.

She took a look around. The town reminded her of Bear Creek, but the Bear Creek of ten years ago, when she had first arrived in Oscar and Sarah's care.

Half of the buildings looked as if they had seen better days. Worn boards, peeling paint, dingy windows facing the main street. The other half showed that someone had been putting work into them. They were in good repair with a fresh coat of colorful paint that made the more worn buildings look even worse.

She straightened her shoulders and faced the school building that doubled as the church on Sunday mornings. She'd gotten that much information when she'd received an invitation to interview. She'd been promised nothing else.

If she managed to get the job, she would have to figure out transportation. She couldn't ask her father to take a full day away from his work on the ranch when she needed to return home once a month or so. And she wasn't great at driving a buggy. She could maybe make it from the homestead to town, but there was no way she could drive six hours across the wild country. And she couldn't imagine staying here for nine months without seeing her family.

But she wasn't sure she needed to worry. If she didn't get this job, she might be at home for the foreseeable future.

Her hand trembled on the doorknob as she turned it and entered the schoolhouse.

Inside, the schoolhouse had been completely revitalized. The desks were new and clean, the chalkboard almost shining. There was an entire bookshelf on one wall —*filled* with books!

Two men waited inside, standing near the teacher's desk.

She put on her best smile and went to meet them.

Mr. Collins had a mustache that quivered when he spoke. It was so big that she couldn't tell whether he was smiling or frowning.

Mr. Tellers was thin and tall with graying hair.

"Mr. Morgan is the third school board member," Mr. Tellers said. "He's tied up in a meeting and should join us later."

"Let's get down to business," Mr. Collins said.

They asked about her schooling. She told them about her family and about how having so many siblings and cousins had inspired her to teach.

When they asked about her experience teaching last year, she felt her smile slip. She'd finally admitted to Sarah what had happened. Her mother had advised her to speak the truth.

So Cecilia did. She explained about the misunderstanding and was earnest as she told them that she had no intention of letting a situation like that happen again.

She'd learned her lesson well. She would allow no more mistakes.

After what had happened with Simon, she wouldn't trust a man with her reputation.

"I never intend to marry," she told them. "And I won't put myself in any situation where my morals could be questioned."

She couldn't tell whether her words had any effect. The two men remained serious, almost grave.

They concluded the interview—still no sign of Mr. Morgan—and Sarah rose from the desk where she'd perched. It would be after dark before she and Papa arrived home.

She let herself imagine for one moment that this was her classroom. What would it be like filled with children, curious and eager to learn?

She wanted it.

She was halfway across the schoolroom when the outside door opened. A man stepped inside, and Cecilia froze.

She'd never, not in her entire life, seen such a fine specimen of a man. He had a hat in one hand, and his uncovered hair was perfectly golden blond. Even the faint hint of stubble on his cheeks was golden, and when it might've looked disreputable on another man, it only served to make this man, whoever he was, even more handsome.

His eyes were light blue, a shade she'd only read about in books. He wore a fancy jacket, the cut of which revealed a chest thick with muscle. The same kind of muscles her uncles had—the kind one built from hours and hours of hard work.

She realized he was saying something. It took her one slow blink to snap back into the moment.

His gaze was warm, and his eyes crinkled slightly at the corners.

Flustered, she glanced down at the floor. The moment her eyes broke contact, she came to herself.

She'd just finished telling the school board members that she was respectable. That they could trust her with their children, and that she would be respectable.

And the very next thing she'd done was to ogle the first handsome man that had come along.

What had she been thinking? She hadn't.

She realized she missed the entirety of he'd said.

Her face burned. She clasped her hands tightly in front of her. "I'm terribly sorry. What did you say?"

He smiled. And if she'd thought him handsome before, well, it was nothing compared to seeing him smile.

Her stomach fell like it had the time she'd watched her toddler brother jump from the barn window into a pile of hay below.

She blinked.

"I was only apologizing for my tardiness. I can only hope you won't hold it against me if we are to work together this school term."

A sound like rushing water filled her ears.

Work together?

For a school of only twelve students, there would be no need for more than one teacher.

He took a step closer and stretched out his hand. "I am John Morgan. Chairman of the school board."

No.

Oh no.

ALSO BY LACY WILLIAMS

Wind River Hearts series

Marrying Miss Marshal

Counterfeit Cowboy

Cowboy Pride

The Homesteader's Sweetheart

Courted by a Cowboy

Roping the Wrangler

Return of the Cowboy Doctor

The Wrangler's Inconvenient Wife

A Cowboy for Christmas

Her Convenient Cowboy

Her Cowboy Deputy

Catching the Cowgirl

The Cowboy's Honor

Sutter's Hollow series (contemporary romance)

His Small-Town Girl

Secondhand Cowboy

The Cowgirl Next Door

Looking Back, Texas series (contemporary romance)

10 Dates

Next Door Santa

Always a Bridesmaid

Love Lessons

The Sawyer Creek series (contemporary romance)

Soldier Under the Mistletoe

The Nanny's Christmas Wish

The Rancher's Unexpected Gift

Someone Old

Someone New

Someone Borrowed

Someone Blue (newsletter subscribers only)

The Bull Rider

The Brother

The Prodigal

Cowboy Fairytales series (contemporary romance)

Once Upon a Cowboy

Cowboy Charming

The Toad Prince

The Beastly Princess

The Lost Princess

Kissing Kelsey

Courting Carrie

Stealing Sarah

Keeping Kayla

Melting Megan

Heart of Oklahoma series (contemporary romance)

Kissed by a Cowboy

Love Letters from Cowboy

Mistletoe Cowboy

Cowgirl for Keeps

Jingle Bell Cowgirl

Heart of a Cowgirl

3 Days with a Cowboy

Prodigal Cowgirl

Not in a Series

Wagon Train Sweetheart (historical romance)

Printed in Great Britain
by Amazon

23429453R00142